THE FOLGER LIBRARY
SHAKESPEARE

Designed to make Shakespeare's classic plays available to the general reader, each edition contains a reliable text with modernized spelling and punctuation

The Folger Shakespeare Library

The Folger Shakespeare Library in Washington, D.C., a research institute founded and endowed by Henry Clay Folger and administered by the Trustees of Amherst College, contains the world's largest collection of Shakespeareana. Although the Folger Library's primary purpose is to encourage advanced research in history and literature, it has continually exhibited a profound concern in stimulating a popular interest in the Elizabethan period.

GENERAL EDITOR

LOUIS B. WRIGHT

Director, Folger Shakespeare Library, 1948–1968

ASSISTANT EDITOR

VIRGINIA A. LaMAR

Executive Secretary, Folger Shakespeare Library, 1946–1968

The Folger Library General Reader's Shakespeare

Troilus and Cressida

by

WILLIAM SHAKESPEARE

WASHINGTON SQUARE PRESS
PUBLISHED BY POCKET BOOKS
New York   London   Toronto   Sydney   Tokyo   Singapore

A Washington Square Press Publication of
POCKET BOOKS, a division of Simon & Schuster, Inc.
1230 Avenue of the Americas, New York, N.Y. 10020

ISBN: 0-671-66916-8

First Pocket Books printing July 1966

10 9 8 7 6 5

WASHINGTON SQUARE PRESS and WSP colophon are registered trademarks of Simon & Schuster, Inc.

Printed in the U.S.A.

Preface

This edition of *Troilus and Cressida* is designed to make
available a readable text of an enigmatic play that has
defied precise classification, but which contains one of
the clearest expressions of Shakespeare's social philosophy to be found in any of his dramas. In the centuries
since Shakespeare, many changes have occurred in the
meanings of words, and some clarification of Shakespeare's vocabulary may be helpful. To provide the
reader with necessary notes in the most accessible
format, we have placed them on the pages facing the
text that they explain. We have tried to make these
notes as brief and simple as possible. Preliminary to the
text we have also included a brief statement of essential
information about Shakespeare and his stage. Readers
desiring more detailed information should refer to
the books suggested in the references, and if still further
information is needed, the bibliographies in those books
will provide the necessary clues to the literature of the
subject.

The early texts of Shakespeare's plays provide only
scattered stage directions and no indications of setting,
and it is conventional for modern editors to add these
to clarify the action. Such additions, and additions to
entrances and exits, as well as many indications of act
and scene division, are placed in square brackets.

All illustrations are from material in the Folger
Library collections.

L. B. W.
V. A. L.

August 20, 1965

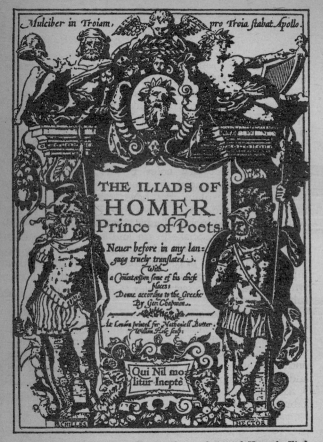

Mulciber in Troiam.   pro Troia stabat Apollo.

THE ILIADS OF
HOMER
Prince of Poets

Neuer before in any lan=
guag truely translated.
With
a Co[m]ent vppon some of his chiefe
places;
Donne according to the Greeke
By Geo. Chapman

At London printed for Nathaniell Butter
William Hole sculp:

Qui Nil mo=
litur Ineptè

ACHILLES   HECTOR

The title page of George Chapman's translation of Homer's *Iliad*
(?1611).

A Satire on Romantic Heroics

In *Troilus and Cressida* Shakespeare wrote a play
that has puzzled critics, who have found it difficult
to classify in any known category. In *Hamlet*
Polonius announced that the strolling players who
came to Elsinore were the "best actors in the world,
either for tragedy, comedy, history, pastoral,
pastoral-comical, historical-pastoral, tragical-histori-
cal, tragical-comical-historical-pastoral," or any
other type of drama. But Polonius, for all of this
medley of dramatic types, forgot to specify a
classification that would precisely fit the kind of
play that Shakespeare was soon to write, for
Troilus and Cressida is not the conventional type of
comedy, tragedy, or history, though, to the Elizabethans, it had in it a little of all three elements.

Shakespeare's own contemporaries were clearly
troubled about where to classify the play; at one
time they called it a "history" and at another, a
"tragedy." The editors of the First Folio of 1623
apparently first intended to include it among the
tragedies, for in two copies of the Folio the first leaf
of *Troilus and Cressida* appears after *Romeo and
Juliet* among the tragedies. Something happened to
prevent its inclusion at this point, and *Timon of
Athens* was substituted. Later, *Troilus and Cressida*

was placed, in an insertion without pagination, between the histories and the tragedies. This compromise—if it was that—has not pleased later critics, who like to have works neatly classified; *Troilus and Cressida*, however, defies such classification. The play is a dramatic satire that has both tragic and comic elements; the Elizabethans, who thought of the Trojan War as a genuine episode in ancient history, probably regarded *Troilus and Cressida* as a chronicle play as well. Whatever it is, it contains material that has attracted the interest of readers from Shakespeare's day to our own.

The best evidence indicates that *Troilus and Cressida* was first performed sometime in 1602, which would place it several years after such romantic and lyrical plays as *Romeo and Juliet* and *Richard II*, after the romantic comedies, after *Hamlet*, and just before *All's Well That Ends Well* and *Measure for Measure*. The year 1602 was not a period of romantic lyricism in the career of William Shakespeare or in the history of England. On the contrary, it was a time of satirical commentary, of uncertainty and cynicism, all of which finds reflection in the drama.

One of the most popular dramatists of the day was Ben Jonson, whose corrosive comedies brought before their audiences a great parade of fools and knaves treated satirically. No longer was romantic drama in style. During this period satiric plays swept all before them, and every acting company had to keep up with the fashion. It was only natural that Shakespeare, who was always aware of shifting tastes in the theatre, should have contributed a play in the style that current taste demanded. Shakespeare was ever the practical playwright, always ready to supply what his company required.

But *Troilus and Cressida* is something more than a play written merely to satisfy the needs of the Lord Chamberlain's Men for a fashionable satire. It shows evidence of the author's own emotional maturity and his philosophic concern with problems of social relationships. In the words of Professor Virgil Whitaker, *Troilus and Cressida* is "Shakespeare's own key to his greatest plays" and is "a powerful, if unconventional, mirror of human nature."

Inevitably the love of Romeo for Juliet will be compared with that of Troilus for Cressida. Both pairs of lovers undergo analogous experiences—but with a difference. In the earlier play, Shakespeare treats lyrically young and innocent love. Romeo and Juliet are moved by sexual passion, it is true, but Shakespeare sees to it that they are legally married by Friar Laurence before the consummation of their love. In the later play, Shakespeare deals realistically with more mature lovers. They too are swept along by sexual passion, but Shakespeare no longer requires for them the benefit of clergy or of lyric verse; instead, he creates a go-between to arrange, in prosy dialogue, for their first assignation. The situation reads like a travesty of the parallel action in *Romeo and Juliet*.

Yet the love scenes in *Troilus and Cressida* are not a burlesque of human emotion, and Cressida, for all of her shortcomings, is not a mere abstraction of Infidelity. To Bernard Shaw, at any rate, Cressida was "Shakespeare's first real woman." In this play, Shakespeare is dealing with another aspect of love —an aspect common in real life, then as now. Many a woman—or man—has vowed eternal fidelity and then found temptation too strong to resist, once the object of the vow was out of sight. As Shakespeare knew, this is a common situation in life, and he made his pair of lovers human beings recognizable as realistic types.

Other more profound problems find expression in the play. In the broadest sense, *Troilus and Cressida* is a political commentary on the times. Some scholars have been tempted to see a precise parallel between the situation in the Grecian camp and conditions in England during the period of the Earl of Essex' quarrel with the Queen and his subsequent rebellion. Such an interpretation, however, raises many problems and runs contrary to Shakespeare's methods—and his prudence. He would not have been so unwise as to put his neck in a noose by writing a thinly disguised political allegory certain to bring down upon his head the wrath of the authorities. But, in a deeper sense, the play is political, for it discusses the problem of authority in the state and the relation of members of society to the body politic.

The social sickness in the Greek camp, Shakespeare is careful to point out, results from the failure of Agamemnon to exert a strong hand and to discipline his unruly young warriors. In the year before the old Queen's death, many people in England were disturbed over a similar laxness at the center of authority, and they looked to the future with misgivings. Ever lurking in the minds of thoughtful Elizabethans was the fear of disorder in the state. Men living in 1602 could remember the rebellion of the northern earls near the beginning of Queen Elizabeth's reign; many knew about the machinations to place Mary Queen of Scots on the throne of England; the recent rebellion of the Earl of Essex was an ill omen of what might happen again; all literate Englishmen were familiar with written and dramatized histories of the Wars of the Roses; and everyone was aware that Queen Elizabeth could not live forever and that inevitably the time was drawing near when England would have another sovereign. What the future held was a mystery that not even wily Robert Cecil, the Queen's chief minister, could discern, and all men were concerned about the stability of society.

The political and psychological state of England in 1602 gave particular point to Shakespeare's portrayal of the low state of morale in the Greek camp, the frictions that disturbed the harmony of the Greek leaders and impaired their capacity to carry on the war against Troy. Shakespeare did not have to state the moral of his tale or make a parallel with particular individuals in England. Spectators at the performance or readers of the text of the play would see the relevance at once without being told.

Like most of his contemporaries, Shakespeare accepted without question the doctrine of degree in society as necessary to the health of the state. Notions of egalitarianism might addle the brains of a few Anabaptists and other eccentrics, but sensi-

ble Elizabethans subscribed to the idea that a stable
society required the recognition of a hierarchy of
rank and degree. Nowhere is there a better revela-
tion of this belief than in Ulysses' great address to
Agamemnon (I, iii):

> Degree being vizarded,
> The unworthiest shows as fairly in the mask.
> The Heavens themselves, the planets, and this
>   center
> Observe degree, priority, and place,
> Insisture, course, proportion, season, form,
> Office, and custom, in all line of order:
> And therefore is the glorious planet Sol
> In noble eminence enthroned and sphered
> Amidst the other; whose med'cinable eye
> Corrects the ill aspects of planets evil,
> And posts like the commandment of a king,
> Sans check, to good and bad. But when the
>   planets
> In evil mixture to disorder wander,
> What plagues and what portents, what mutiny,
> What raging of the sea, shaking of earth,
> Commotion in the winds, frights, changes, hor-
>   rors,
> Divert and crack, rend and deracinate
> The unity and married calm of states
> Quite from their fixure! Oh, when degree is
>   shaked,
> Which is the ladder to all high designs,
> The enterprise is sick! How could communities,
> Degrees in schools and brotherhoods in cities,
> Peaceful commerce from dividable shores,

The primogenity and due of birth,
Prerogative of age, crowns, scepters, laurels,
But by degree, stand in authentic place?
Take but degree away, untune that string,
And hark what discord follows. Each thing
    meets
In mere oppugnancy. The bounded waters
Should lift their bosoms higher than the shores
And make a sop of all this solid globe;
Strength should be lord of imbecility,
And the rude son should strike his father dead;
Force should be right, or rather, right and
    wrong,
Between whose endless jar justice resides,
Should lose their names, and so should justice
    too.
Then everything includes itself in power,
Power into will, will into appetite;
And appetite, an universal wolf,
So doubly seconded with will and power,
Must make perforce an universal prey,
And last eat up himself. Great Agamemnon,
This chaos, when degree is suffocate,
Follows the choking.
And this neglection of degree it is
That by a pace goes backward, with a purpose
It hath to climb. The general's disdained
By him one step below; he by the next;
That next by him beneath: so every step,
Exampled by the first pace that is sick
Of his superior, grows to an envious fever
Of pale and bloodless emulation.
And 'tis this fever that keeps Troy on foot,

Not her own sinews. To end a tale of length,
Troy in our weakness stands, not in her strength.

This speech is written with such intensity and obvious sincerity that it serves as the keynote to the political lessons of the play. Anything that disturbs the ordered condition of society is evil, Shakespeare continues to drive home, whether it be Paris' abduction of Helen, Troilus' passion for Cressida, or Achilles' prima-donnaish behavior that leaves him sulking in his tent when he ought to be in the field.

Although *Troilus and Cressida* concerns itself with war, indeed with chivalric episodes that had entertained readers of the Troy legends for centuries past, Shakespeare is no longer concerned with romantic heroics. Present-day readers of *Troilus and Cressida* find much to interest them in this play, because Shakespeare sounds so "modern." For him war is no longer an occasion for glamorous deeds or patriotic oratory. The spirit expressed in *Henry V* and the other history plays finds no echo in *Troilus and Cressida*. The whole bloody business of war is not only stupid, but it is a bore, Shakespeare is saying. As if to give emphasis to the unheroic quality of the military episodes, Shakespeare makes the foul-mouthed Thersites serve as a sort of Chorus commenting on the action.

Critics of this play have not sufficiently recognized the dramatic and theatrical qualities of Thersites. Shakespeare, always mindful of theatrical requirements, lavishes a great deal of care upon his clowns, and Thersites serves the place of a clown, a surly and bitter clown to be sure, but a comic commentator on the action, who points up the ideas that Shakespeare is intent upon emphasizing. In a somewhat similar fashion, the clown in *King Lear*, written a few years later, serves as a choral commentary upon the old king's behavior.

The question of the audience for whom Shakespeare designed *Troilus and Cressida* has troubled scholars. Its tone is that of the satirical plays written by Marston, Dekker, Jonson, and others and acted in the various London playhouses. Shakespeare would have been expected by his company to turn out a play in the current fashion for the Lord Chamberlain's Men. As a matter of fact, an entry in the Stationers' Register for February 7, 1603, licensing the play to the printer James Roberts, described it as "The book of *Troilus and Cressida* as it is acted by my Lord Chamberlain's Men." In 1609, the play was published in Quarto by Richard Bonian and Henry Walley as *The History of Troilus and Cressida. As It Was Acted by the King's Majesty's Servants at the Globe. Written by William Shakespeare.* Shakespeare's company had by this time changed its name from the Lord Chamberlain's Men to the King's Men, for the new sovereign, King James, had taken them under his protection. Later in the year 1609, before Bonian and Walley disposed of all copies of the Quarto, they had printed up a new title page which read: *The Famous History of Troilus and Cressida. Excellently Expressing the Beginning of Their Loves, with the Conceited Wooing of Pandarus, Prince of Licia. Written by William Shakespeare.* Included in this issue was a preface headed, "A never writer to an ever reader: news," and beginning:

Eternal reader, you have here a new play, never staled with the stage, never clapperclawed with the palms of the vulgar, and yet passing full of the palm comical; for it is a birth of your [Shakespeare's] brain that never undertook anything comical vainly. And were but the vain names of comedies changed for the titles of commodities, or of plays for pleas, you should see all those grand censors that now style them such vanities flock to them for the main grace of their gravities; especially this author's comedies, that are so framed to the life that they serve for the most common commentaries of all the actions of our lives, showing such a dexterity and power of wit that the most displeased with plays are pleased with his comedies.

The wording of this preface, with puns on legal terms, suggests that it was intended for one of the Inns of Court. The publishers may have prepared this issue of the Quarto for a revival at one of the Inns of Court and wanted to make it appear that the play had never before been acted on a public stage. In view of the statement in 1603 that it had been acted by the Lord Chamberlain's Men, and the assertion in the first issue of the Quarto of 1609 that it had been acted at the Globe, the subsequent effort to show that it had never before been acted in a public playhouse is open to grave suspicion. Of course it is not impossible that it was first acted at Court, or at one of the Inns of Court, where it may have had a later revival. It is possible to interpret "never clapperclawed with the palms of the vulgar" as meaning that it was not a success with the multitude, a statement intended to flatter an audience presumably capable of appreciating the play.

This preface emphasizes the appeal of Shakespeare's comedies and by implication classifies *Troilus and Cressida* as one of his "witty" comedies. Clearly the author of this preface thought of it as a play analogous to the satirical comedies that were popular at the turn of the century and a few years after. Coming as this play does just before the writing of the somewhat bitter problem comedies, *All's Well That Ends Well* and *Measure for Measure*, *Troilus and Cressida* may be properly classed with them. But it makes little difference whether we can find a neat pigeonhole into which we can fit the play. It is a work of art, as well as a work of philosophic and political importance. It is a play worth careful study, for it has depths of meaning that escape a casual reading.

In *Troilus and Cressida* Shakespeare displays an experimental vein reflected in the structure of the play, the treatment of his theme, and the language that he uses. The play contains many Latinate words that appear in English for the first time, evidently adapted by Shakespeare. Examples are *corresponsive, conflux, tortive, protractive, persistive, insisture, attributive, assubjugate, repured, embrasures, deceptious.*

The theme of the Trojan War was exceedingly

popular in Shakespeare's day, and his was not the only play on the subject. The rival company, the Lord Admiral's Men, controlled by Philip Henslowe, in 1596 staged a play listed as *Troy;* three years later Henslowe hired Henry Chettle and Thomas Dekker to write another play which he set down in his account book simply as "troyless and creseda." Long before this date, interludes had used episodes from the Matter of Troy; and an interlude entitled *Thersites* dates from 1562. Trojan material was common in drama, fiction, and narrative poetry. One reason for its popularity was the belief that Englishmen were "true Trojans," that London had been founded by Brutus, the great-grandson of Aeneas, and that the English nation had sprung from this noble Trojan.

Shakespeare had ample sources to draw upon, and the origins of his own version of the Troilus and Cressida story are complex. Gilbert Highet, in *The Classical Tradition,* points out that the play is "a dramatization of part of a translation into English of the French translation of a Latin imitation of an old French expansion of a Latin epitome of a Greek romance." The easiest source of the Troilus story for Shakespeare, as well as for other Elizabethans, was Chaucer's *Troilus and Criseyde,* available in several editions of Chaucer's *Works.* Chaucer himself had drawn on various sources, including two Latin narratives that were popular in the Middle Ages: *Ephemerides Belli Trojani,* attributed to one Dictys Cretensis, and *Historia de excidio Trojae,* attributed to Dares Phrygius. The story passed into the vernacular literature of France through Benoît de

Sainte-More's *Roman de Troie,* from which Guido delle Colonne made a Latin version called *Historia destructionis Trojae.* Boccaccio used a version of the Troilus story in his own *Filostrato,* based on the preceding authors, and Chaucer used Boccaccio. Besides Chaucer, Shakespeare derived incidents from Caxton's *Recuyell of the Historyes of Troye* and probably from John Lydgate's *Sege of Troye,* both of which contain Grecian episodes not found in Chaucer. A Scottish poet, Robert Henryson, wrote a sequel to Chaucer, entitled *The Testament of Cresseid,* which told of the sad end of Cressida as a prostitute in a house of lepers. Shakespeare knew Henryson's work, which was included in some editions of Chaucer without credit to Henryson.

Knowledge of the Trojan War was also available in George Chapman's translations of Homer's *Iliad,* which began to appear in 1598. An older translation of ten books of the *Iliad* by Arthur Hall, published in 1581, may have been known to Shakespeare. Besides these sources, various poems and several earlier plays utilizing the Trojan theme may have suggested details to Shakespeare. Few literary subjects were more familiar to the Elizabethans than the stories of the Greeks and the Trojans.

The stage history of *Troilus and Cressida* is scanty. Since virtually nothing is known about its performances in Shakespeare's own time, the conclusion is that it was not a stage success. After the Restoration and the reopening of the theatres in 1660, *Troilus and Cressida* was not one of Shakespeare's plays chosen for immediate performance, but by 1679 John Dryden got around to making an adaptation of it with the title *Troilus and Cressida, or Truth Found Too Late*. As a stage production, Dryden's version improves on Shakespeare, because he recast the play so that it had a discernible structure. He made his adaptation into a tragedy. Cressida is a virtuous heroine, faithful to Troilus, who learns too late of her complete fidelity. Indeed, Cressida has to kill herself to convince him. Diomedes is the villain of the piece. Though a modern audience may not relish Cressida's demonstration of virtue, Hazelton Spencer comments of Dryden's play that "at least Dryden gives the play an ending." Shakespeare had left the action dangling.

Dryden's version had no great popularity, and after it for two centuries a vast silence closes upon *Troilus and Cressida*. The eighteenth and nineteenth centuries let the play severely alone. No performances are recorded until 1898, when it was revived in Germany in a Munich theatre. Berlin saw another performance in 1904. It was revived in London in 1907. Since then, the play has had a number of performances, possibly because it does reflect something of the modern attitude toward war and romantic heroics in general. The Old Vic Company made it part of its repertory and gave a successful performance in Edwardian dress in 1956. The American Shakespeare Festival Company at Stratford, Connecticut, staged the play in 1961 in Civil War costume, with the Trojans uniformed as Confederate soldiers and the Greeks clothed like the Union forces. The most recent production was that of the New York Shakespeare Festival in 1965.

NOTE ON THE TEXT

The present edition uses the Quarto version as the basis of its text, but, like most modern editions, it takes readings from the Folio of 1623 when those readings seem to make better sense. The Quarto provides a good text, perhaps printed from the author's manuscript. The Folio appears to have been printed from a Quarto corrected from another manuscript, perhaps the playhouse copy. The Folio has a number of passages which do not appear in the Quarto at all (including the Prologue); these have been incorporated in the present edition.

THE AUTHOR

As early as 1598 Shakespeare was so well known as a literary and dramatic craftsman that Francis Meres, in his *Palladis Tamia: Wits Treasury*, referred in flattering terms to him as "mellifluous and honey-tongued Shakespeare," famous for his *Venus and Adonis*, his *Lucrece*, and "his sugared sonnets," which were circulating "among his private friends." Meres observes further that "as Plautus and Seneca are accounted the best for comedy and tragedy among the Latins, so Shakespeare among the English is the most excellent in both kinds for the stage," and he mentions a dozen plays that had made a name for Shakespeare. He concludes with the remark that "the Muses would speak with Shakespeare's fine filed phrase if they would speak English."

To those acquainted with the history of the Elizabethan and Jacobean periods, it is incredible that anyone should be so naïve or ignorant as to doubt the reality of Shakespeare as the author of the plays that bear his name. Yet so much nonsense has been written about other "candidates" for the plays that it is well to remind readers that no credible evidence that would stand up in a court of law has ever been adduced to prove either that Shakespeare did not write his plays or that anyone else wrote them. All the theories offered for the authorship of Francis Bacon, the Earl of Derby, the Earl of Oxford, the Earl of Hertford, Christopher Marlowe, and a score of other candidates are mere conjectures spun from the active imaginations of persons who confuse hypothesis and conjecture with evidence.

As Meres's statement of 1598 indicates, Shakespeare was already a popular playwright whose name carried weight at the box office. The obvious reputation of Shakespeare as early as 1598 makes the effort to prove him a myth one of the most absurd in the history of human perversity.

The anti-Shakespeareans talk darkly about a plot of vested interests to maintain the authorship of Shakespeare. Nobody has any vested interest in Shakespeare, but every scholar is interested in the truth and in the quality of evidence advanced by special pleaders who set forth hypotheses in place of facts.

The anti-Shakespeareans base their arguments upon a few simple premises, all of them false. The false premises are that Shakespeare was an unlettered yokel without any schooling, that nothing is known about Shakespeare, and that only a noble lord or the equivalent in background could have written the plays. The facts are that more is known about Shakespeare than about most dramatists of his day, that he had a very good education, acquired in the Stratford Grammar School, that the plays show no evidence of profound book learning, and that the knowledge of kings and courts evident in the plays is no greater than any intelligent young man could have picked up at second hand. Most anti-Shakespeareans are naïve and betray an obvious snobbery. The author of their favorite plays, they imply, must have had a college diploma framed and hung on his study wall like the one in their dentist's office, and obviously so great a writer must have had a title or some equally significant evidence of exalted social background. They forget that genius has a way of cropping up in unexpected places and that none of the great creative writers of the world got his inspiration in a college or university course.

William Shakespeare was the son of John Shakespeare of Stratford-upon-Avon, a substantial citizen of that small but busy market town in the center of the rich agricultural county of Warwick. John Shakespeare kept a shop, what we would call a general store; he dealt in wool and other produce and gradually acquired property. As a youth, John Shakespeare had learned the trade of glover and leather worker. There is no contemporary evidence that the elder Shakespeare was a butcher, though the anti-Shakespeareans like to talk about the ignorant "butcher's boy of Stratford." Their only evidence is a statement by gossipy John Aubrey, more than a century after William Shakespeare's birth, that young William followed his father's trade, and when he killed a calf, "he would do it in a high style and make a speech." We would like to believe the story true, but Aubrey is not a very credible witness.

John Shakespeare probably continued to operate a farm at Snitterfield that his father had leased. He married Mary Arden, daughter of his father's landlord, a man of some property. The third of their eight children was William, baptized on April 26, 1564, and probably born three days before. At least, it is conventional to celebrate April 23 as his birthday.

The Stratford records give considerable information about John Shakespeare. We know that he held several municipal offices including those of alderman and mayor. In 1580 he was in some sort of legal difficulty and was fined for neglecting a summons of the Court of Queen's Bench requiring him to appear at Westminster and be bound over to keep the peace.

As a citizen and alderman of Stratford, John Shakespeare was entitled to send his son to the grammar school free. Though the records are lost, there can be no reason to doubt that this is where young William received his education. As any student of the period knows, the grammar schools provided the basic education in Latin learning and literature. The Elizabethan grammar school is not to be confused with modern grammar schools. Many

cultivated men of the day received all their formal
education in the grammar schools. At the universities in this period a student would have received
little training that would have inspired him to be a
creative writer. At Stratford young Shakespeare
would have acquired a familiarity with Latin and
some little knowledge of Greek. He would have
read Latin authors and become acquainted with
the plays of Plautus and Terence. Undoubtedly, in
this period of his life he received that stimulation
to read and explore for himself the world of ancient
and modern history which he later utilized in his
plays. The youngster who does not acquire this
type of intellectual curiosity *before* college days
rarely develops as a result of a college course the
kind of mind Shakespeare demonstrated. His learning in books was anything but profound, but he
clearly had the probing curiosity that sent him in
search of information, and he had a keenness in the
observation of nature and of humankind that finds
reflection in his poetry.

There is little documentation for Shakespeare's
boyhood. There is little reason why there should
be. Nobody knew that he was going to be a dramatist about whom any scrap of information would be
prized in the centuries to come. He was merely an
active and vigorous youth of Stratford, perhaps as-
sisting his father in his business, and no Boswell
bothered to write down facts about him. The most
important record that we have is a marriage license
issued by the Bishop of Worcester on November
27, 1582, to permit William Shakespeare to marry
Anne Hathaway, seven or eight years his senior;

furthermore, the Bishop permitted the marriage after reading the banns only once instead of three times, evidence of the desire for haste. The need was explained on May 26, 1583, when the christening of Susanna, daughter of William and Anne Shakespeare, was recorded at Stratford. Two years later, on February 2, 1585, the records show the birth of twins to the Shakespeares, a boy and a girl who were christened Hamnet and Judith.

What William Shakespeare was doing in Stratford during the early years of his married life, or when he went to London, we do not know. It has been conjectured that he tried his hand at schoolteaching, but that is a mere guess. There is a legend that he left Stratford to escape a charge of poaching in the park of Sir Thomas Lucy of Charlecote, but there is no proof of this. There is also a legend that when first he came to London he earned his living by holding horses outside a playhouse and presently was given employment inside, but there is nothing better than eighteenth-century hearsay for this. How Shakespeare broke into the London theatres as a dramatist and actor we do not know. But lack of information is not surprising, for Elizabethans did not write their autobiographies, and we know even less about the lives of many writers and some men of affairs than we know about Shakespeare. By 1592 he was so well established and popular that he incurred the envy of the dramatist and pamphleteer Robert Greene, who referred to him as an "upstart crow . . . in his own conceit the only Shake-scene in a country." From this time onward, contemporary allusions and references in legal documents enable the scholar to chart Shakespeare's career with greater accuracy than is possible with most other Elizabethan dramatists.

By 1594 Shakespeare was a member of the company of actors known as the Lord Chamberlain's Men. After the accession of James I, in 1603, the company would have the sovereign for its patron and would be known as the King's Men. During the period of its greatest prosperity, this company would have as its principal theatres the Globe and the Blackfriars. Shakespeare was both an actor and a shareholder in the company. Tradition has assigned him such acting roles as Adam in *As You Like It* and the Ghost in *Hamlet,* a modest place on the stage that suggests that he may have had other duties in the management of the company. Such conclusions, however, are based on surmise.

What we do know is that his plays were popular and that he was highly successful in his vocation. His first play may have been *The Comedy of Errors,* acted perhaps in 1591. Certainly this was one of his earliest plays. The three parts of *Henry VI* were acted sometime between 1590 and 1592. Critics are not in agreement about precisely how much Shakespeare wrote of these three plays. *Richard III* probably dates from 1593. With this play Shakespeare captured the imagination of Elizabethan audiences, then enormously interested in historical plays. With *Richard III* Shakespeare also gave an interpretation pleasing to the Tudors of the rise to power of the grandfather of Queen Elizabeth. From this time onward, Shakespeare's plays followed on the stage in rapid succession: *Titus Andronicus, The Taming of the Shrew, The Two Gentlemen of Verona, Love's Labor's Lost, Romeo and Juliet, Richard II, A Midsummer Night's Dream, King John, The Merchant of Venice, Henry IV (Parts 1 and 2), Much Ado about Nothing, Henry V, Julius Cæsar, As You Like It, Twelfth Night, Hamlet, The Merry Wives of Windsor, All's Well That Ends Well, Measure for Measure, Othello, King Lear*, and nine others that followed before Shakespeare retired completely, about 1613.

In the course of his career in London, he made enough money to enable him to retire to Stratford with a competence. His purchase on May 4, 1597, of New Place, then the second-largest dwelling in Stratford, a "pretty house of brick and timber," with a handsome garden, indicates his increasing prosperity. There his wife and children lived while he busied himself in the London theatres. The summer before he acquired New Place, his life was darkened by the death of his only son, Hamnet, a child of eleven. In May, 1602, Shakespeare purchased one hundred and seven acres of fertile farmland near Stratford and a few months later bought a cottage and garden across the alley from New Place. About 1611, he seems to have returned permanently to Stratford, for the next year a legal document refers to him as "William Shakespeare of Stratford-upon-Avon . . . gentleman." To achieve the desired appellation of gentleman, William Shakespeare had seen to it that the College of Heralds in 1596 granted his father a coat of arms. In one step he thus became a second-generation gentleman.

Shakespeare's daughter Susanna made a good match in 1607 with Dr. John Hall, a prominent and prosperous Stratford physician. His second daughter, Judith, did not marry until she was thirty-one years old, and then, under somewhat scandalous circumstances, she married Thomas Quiney, a Stratford vintner. On March 25, 1616, Shakespeare made his will, bequeathing his landed property to Susanna, £300 to Judith, certain sums to other relatives, and his second-best bed to his wife, Anne. Much has been made of the second-best bed, but the legacy probably indicates only that Anne liked that particular bed. Shakespeare, following the practice of the time, may have already arranged with Susanna for his wife's care. Finally, on April 23, 1616, the anniversary of his birth, William Shakespeare died, and he was buried on April 25 within the chancel of Trinity Church, as befitted an honored citizen. On August 6, 1623, a few months before the publication of the collected edition of Shakespeare's plays, Anne Shakespeare joined her husband in death.

THE PUBLICATION OF HIS PLAYS

During his lifetime Shakespeare made no effort to publish any of his plays, though eighteen appeared in print in single-play editions known as Quartos. Some of these are corrupt versions known as "bad Quartos." No Quarto, so far as is known, had the author's approval. Plays were not considered "literature" any more than most radio and television scripts today are considered literature. Dramatists sold their plays outright to the theatrical companies and it was usually considered in the company's interest to keep plays from getting into print. To achieve a reputation as a man of letters, Shakespeare wrote his *Sonnets* and his narrative poems, *Venus and Adonis* and *The Rape of Lucrece*, but he probably never dreamed that his plays would establish his reputation as a literary genius. Only Ben Jonson, a man known for his colossal conceit, had the crust to call his plays *Works*, as he did when he published an edition in 1616. But men laughed at Ben Jonson.

After Shakespeare's death, two of his old colleagues in the King's Men, John Heminges and Henry Condell, decided that it would be a good thing to print, in more accurate versions than were then available, the plays already published and eighteen additional plays not previously published in Quarto. In 1623 appeared *Mr. William Shakespeare's Comedies, Histories, & Tragedies. Published according to the True Original Copies. London. Printed by Isaac Iaggard and Ed. Blount*. This was the famous First Folio, a work that had the authority of Shakespeare's associates. The only play commonly attributed to Shakespeare that was omitted in the First Folio was *Pericles*. In their preface, "To the great Variety of Readers," Heminges and Condell state that whereas "you were abused with diverse stolen and surreptitious copies, maimed and deformed by the frauds and stealths of injurious impostors that exposed them, even those are now offered to your view cured and perfect of their limbs; and all the rest, absolute in their numbers, as he conceived them." What they used for printer's copy is one of the vexed problems of scholarship, and skilled bibliographers have devoted years of study to the question of the relation of the "copy" for the First Folio to Shakespeare's manuscripts. In some cases it is clear that the editors corrected printed Quarto versions of the plays, probably by comparison with playhouse scripts. Whether these scripts were in Shakespeare's autograph is anybody's guess. No manuscript of any play in Shakespeare's handwriting has survived. Indeed, very few play manuscripts from this period by any author are extant. The Tudor and Stuart periods had not yet learned to prize autographs and author's original manuscripts.

Since the First Folio contains eighteen plays not previously printed, it is the only source for these. For the other eighteen, which had appeared in Quarto versions, the First Folio also has the authority of an edition prepared and overseen by Shakespeare's colleagues and professional associates. But since editorial standards in 1623 were far from strict, and Heminges and Condell were actors rather than editors by profession, the texts are sometimes careless. The printing and proofreading of the First Folio also left much to be desired, and some garbled passages have had to be corrected and emended. The "good Quarto" texts have to be taken into account in preparing a modern edition.

Because of the great popularity of Shakespeare through the centuries, the First Folio has become a prized book, but it is not a very rare one, for it is estimated that 238 copies are extant. The Folger Shakespeare Library in Washington, D.C., has seventy-nine copies of the First Folio, collected by the founder, Henry Clay Folger, who believed that a collation of as many texts as possible would reveal significant facts about the text of Shakespeare's plays. Dr. Charlton Hinman, using an ingenious machine of his own invention for mechanical collating, has made many discoveries that throw light on Shakespeare's text and on printing practices of the day.

The probability is that the First Folio of 1623 had an edition of between 1,000 and 1,250 copies. It is believed that it sold for £1, which made it an expensive book, for £1 in 1623 was equivalent to something between $40 and $50 in modern purchasing power.

During the seventeenth century, Shakespeare was sufficiently popular to warrant three later editions in folio size, the Second Folio of 1632, the Third Folio of 1663–1664, and the Fourth Folio of 1685. The Third Folio added six other plays ascribed to Shakespeare, but these are apocryphal.

THE SHAKESPEAREAN THEATRE

The theatres in which Shakespeare's plays were performed were vastly different from those we know today. The stage was a platform that jutted out into the area now occupied by the first rows of seats on the main floor, what is called the "orchestra" in America and the "pit" in England. This platform had no curtain to come down at the ends of acts and scenes. And although simple stage properties were available, the Elizabethan theatre lacked both the machinery and the elaborate movable scenery of the modern theatre. In the rear of the platform stage was a curtained area that could be used as an inner room, a tomb, or any such scene that might be required. A balcony above this inner room, and perhaps balconies on the sides of the stage, could represent the upper deck of a ship, the entry to Juliet's room, or a prison window. A trap door in the stage provided an entrance for ghosts and devils from the nether regions, and a similar trap in the canopied structure over the stage, known as the "heavens," made it possible to let down angels on a rope. These primitive stage arrangements help to account for many elements in Elizabethan plays. For example, since there was no curtain, the dramatist frequently felt the necessity of writing into his play action to clear the stage at the ends of acts and scenes. The funeral march at the end of *Hamlet* is not there merely for atmosphere; Shakespeare had to get the corpses off the stage. The lack of scenery also freed the dramatist from undue concern about the exact location of his sets, and the physical relation of his various settings to each other did not have to be worked out with the same precision as in the modern theatre.

Before London had buildings designed exclusively for theatrical entertainment, plays were given in inns and taverns. The characteristic inn of the period had an inner courtyard with rooms opening onto balconies overlooking the yard. Players could set up their temporary stages at one end of the yard and audiences could find seats on the balconies out of the weather. The poorer sort could stand or sit on the cobblestones in the yard, which was open to the sky. The first theatres followed this construction, and throughout the Elizabethan period the large public theatres had a yard in front of the stage open to the weather, with two or three tiers of covered balconies extending around the theatre. This physical structure again influenced the writing of plays. Because a dramatist wanted the actors to be heard, he frequently wrote into his play orations that could be delivered with declamatory effect. He also provided spectacle, buffoonery, and broad jests to keep the riotous groundlings in the yard entertained and quiet.

In another respect the Elizabethan theatre differed greatly from ours. It had no actresses. All women's roles were taken by boys, sometimes recruited from the boys' choirs of the London churches. Some of these youths acted their roles with great skill and the Elizabethans did not seem to be aware of any incongruity. The first actresses on the professional English stage appeared after the Restoration of Charles II, in 1660, when exiled Englishmen brought back from France practices of the French stage.

London in the Elizabethan period, as now, was the center of theatrical interest, though wandering actors from time to time traveled through the country performing in inns, halls, and the houses of the nobility. The first professional playhouse, called simply The Theatre, was erected by James Burbage, father of Shakespeare's colleague Richard Burbage, in 1576 on lands of the old Holywell Priory adjacent to Finsbury Fields, a playground and park area just north of the city walls. It had the advantage of being outside the city's jurisdiction and yet was near enough to be easily accessible. Soon after The Theatre was opened, another playhouse called The Curtain was erected in the same neighborhood. Both of these playhouses had open courtyards and were probably polygonal in shape.

About the time The Curtain opened, Richard Farrant, Master of the Children of the Chapel Royal at Windsor and St. Paul's, conceived the idea of opening a "private" theatre in the old monastery buildings of the Blackfriars, not far from St. Paul's Cathedral in the heart of the city. This theatre was ostensibly to train the choirboys in plays for presentation at Court, but Farrant managed to present plays to paying audiences and achieved considerable success until aristocratic neighbors complained and had the theatre closed. This first Blackfriars Theatre was significant, however, because it popularized the boy actors in a professional way and it paved the way for a second theatre in the Blackfriars, which Shakespeare's company took over more than thirty years later. By the last years of the sixteenth century, London had at least six professional theatres and still others were erected during the reign of James I.

The Globe Theatre, the playhouse that most people connect with Shakespeare, was erected early in 1599 on the Bankside, the area across the Thames from the city. Its construction had a dramatic beginning, for on the night of December 28, 1598, James Burbage's sons, Cuthbert and Richard, gathered together a crew who tore down the old theatre in Holywell and carted the timbers across the river to a site that they had chosen for a new playhouse. The reason for this clandestine operation was a row with the landowner over the lease to the Holywell property. The site chosen for the Globe was another playground outside of the city's jurisdiction, a region of somewhat unsavory character. Not far away was the Bear Garden, an amphitheatre devoted to the baiting of bears and bulls. This was also the region occupied by many houses of ill fame licensed by the Bishop of Winchester and the source of substantial revenue to him. But it was easily accessible either from London Bridge or by means of the cheap boats operated by the London watermen, and it had the great advantage of being beyond the authority of the Puritanical aldermen of London, who frowned on plays because they lured apprentices from work, filled their heads with improper ideas, and generally exerted a bad influence. The aldermen also complained that the crowds drawn together in the theatre helped to spread the plague.

The Globe was the handsomest theatre up to its time. It was a large building, apparently octagonal in shape, and open like its predecessors to the sky in the center, but capable of seating a large audience in its covered balconies. To erect and operate the Globe, the Burbages organized a syndicate composed of the leading members of the dramatic company, of which Shakespeare was a member.

Since it was open to the weather and depended on natural light, plays had to be given in the afternoon. This caused no hardship in the long afternoons of an English summer, but in the winter the weather was a great handicap and discouraged all except the hardiest. For that reason, in 1608 Shakespeare's company was glad to take over the lease of the second Blackfriars Theatre, a substantial, roomy hall reconstructed within the framework of the old monastery building. This theatre was protected from the weather and its stage was artificially lighted by chandeliers of candles. This became the winter playhouse for Shakespeare's company and at once proved so popular that the congestion of traffic created an embarrassing problem. Stringent regulations had to be made for the movement of coaches in the vicinity. Shakespeare's company continued to use the Globe during the summer months. In 1613 a squib fired from a cannon during a performance of *Henry VIII* fell on the thatched roof and the Globe burned to the ground. The next year it was rebuilt.

London had other famous theatres. The Rose, just west of the Globe, was built by Philip Henslowe, a semiliterate denizen of the Bankside, who became one of the most important theatrical owners and producers of the Tudor and Stuart periods. What is more important for historians, he kept a detailed account book, which provides much of our information about theatrical history in his time. Another famous theatre on the Bankside was the Swan, which a Dutch priest, Johannes de Witt, visited in 1596. The crude drawing of the stage which he made was copied by his friend Arend van Buchell; it is one of the important pieces of contemporary evidence for theatrical construction. Among the other theatres, the Fortune, north of the city, on Golding Lane, and the Red Bull, even farther away from the city, off St. John's Street, were the most popular. The Red Bull, much frequented by apprentices, favored sensational and sometimes rowdy plays.

The actors who kept all of these theatres going were organized into companies under the protection of some noble patron. Traditionally actors had enjoyed a low reputation. In some of the ordinances they were classed as vagrants; in the phraseology of the time, "rogues, vagabonds, sturdy beggars, and common players" were all listed together as undesirables. To escape penalties often meted out to these characters, organized groups of actors managed to gain the protection of various personages of high degree. In the later years of Elizabeth's reign, a group flourished under the name of the Queen's Men; another group had the protection of the Lord Admiral and were known as the Lord Admiral's Men. Edward Alleyn, son-in-law of Philip Henslowe, was the leading spirit in the Lord Admiral's Men. Besides the adult companies, troupes of boy actors from time to time also enjoyed considerable popularity. Among these were the Children of Paul's and the Children of the Chapel Royal.

The company with which Shakespeare had a long association had for its first patron Henry Carey, Lord Hunsdon, the Lord Chamberlain, and hence they were known as the Lord Chamberlain's Men. After the accession of James I, they became the King's Men. This company was the great rival of the Lord Admiral's Men, managed by Henslowe and Alleyn.

All was not easy for the players in Shakespeare's time, for the aldermen of London were always eager for an excuse to close up the Blackfriars and any other theatres in their jurisdiction. The theatres outside the jurisdiction of London were not immune from interference, for they might be shut up by order of the Privy Council for meddling in politics or for various other offenses, or they might be closed in time of plague lest they spread infection. During plague times, the actors usually went on tour and played the provinces wherever they could find an audience. Particularly frightening were the plagues of 1592–1594 and 1613 when the theatres closed and the players, like many other Londoners, had to take to the country.

Though players had a low social status, they enjoyed great popularity, and one of the favorite forms of entertainment at Court was the performance of plays. To be commanded to perform at Court conferred great prestige upon a company of players, and printers frequently noted that fact when they published plays. Several of Shakespeare's plays were performed before the sovereign, and Shakespeare himself undoubtedly acted in some of these plays.

REFERENCES FOR FURTHER READING

Many readers will want suggestions for further reading about Shakespeare and his times. A few references will serve as guides to further study in the enormous literature on the subject. A simple and useful little book is Gerald Sanders, *A Shakespeare Primer* (New York, 1950). *A Companion to Shakespeare Studies,* edited by Harley Granville-Barker and G. B. Harrison (Cambridge, 1934), is a valuable guide. The most recent concise handbook of facts about Shakespeare is Gerald E. Bentley, *Shakespeare: A Biographical Handbook* (New Haven, 1961). More detailed but not so voluminous as to be confusing is Hazelton Spencer, *The Art and Life of William Shakespeare* (New York, 1940), which, like Sanders' and Bentley's handbooks, contains a brief annotated list of useful books on various aspects of the subject. The most detailed and scholarly work providing complete factual information about Shakespeare is Sir Edmund Chambers, *William Shakespeare: A Study of Facts and Problems* (2 vols., Oxford, 1930). Alfred Harbage, *William Shakespeare: A Reader's Guide* (New York, 1963) is a handbook to the reading and appreciation of the plays, with scene synopses and interpretation.

Among other biographies of Shakespeare, Joseph Quincy Adams, *A Life of William Shakespeare* (Boston, 1923) is still an excellent assessment of the essential facts and the traditional information, and Marchette Chute, *Shakespeare of London* (New York, 1949; paperback, 1957) stresses Shakespeare's life in the theatre. Two new biographies of Shakespeare have recently appeared. A. L. Rowse, *William Shakespeare: A Biography* (London, 1963; New York, 1964) provides an appraisal by a distinguished English historian, who dismisses the notion that somebody else wrote Shakespeare's plays as arrant nonsense that runs counter to known historical fact. Peter Quennell, *Shakespeare: A Biography* (Cleveland and New York, 1963) is a sensitive and intelligent survey of what is known and surmised of Shakespeare's life. Louis B. Wright, *Shakespeare for Everyman* (paperback; New York, 1964) discusses the basis of Shakespeare's enduring popularity.

The Shakespeare Quarterly, published by the Shakespeare Association of America under the editorship of James G. McManaway, is recommended for those who wish to keep up with current Shakespearean scholarship and stage productions. The *Quarterly* includes an annual bibliography of Shakespeare editions and works on Shakespeare published during the previous year.

The question of the authenticity of Shakespeare's plays arouses perennial attention. The theory of hidden cryptograms in the plays is demolished by William F. and Elizebeth S. Friedman, *The Shakespearean Ciphers Examined* (New York, 1957). A succinct account of the various absurdities advanced to suggest the authorship of a multitude of candidates other than Shakespeare will be found in R. C. Churchill, *Shakespeare and His Betters* (Bloomington, Ind., 1959). Another recent discussion of the subject, *The Authorship of Shakespeare*, by James

G. McManaway (Washington, D.C., 1962), presents the evidence from contemporary records to prove the identity of Shakespeare the actor-playwright with Shakespeare of Stratford.

Scholars are not in agreement about the details of playhouse construction in the Elizabethan period. John C. Adams presents a plausible reconstruction of the Globe in *The Globe Playhouse: Its Design and Equipment* (Cambridge, Mass., 1942; 2nd rev. ed., 1961). A description with excellent drawings based on Dr. Adams' model is Irwin Smith, *Shakespeare's Globe Playhouse: A Modern Reconstruction in Text and Scale Drawings* (New York, 1956). Other sensible discussions are C. Walter Hodges, *The Globe Restored* (London, 1953), and A. M. Nagler, *Shakespeare's Stage* (New Haven, 1958). Bernard Beckerman, *Shakespeare at the Globe, 1599–1609* (New Haven, 1962; paperback, 1962) discusses Elizabethan staging and acting techniques. Irwin Smith, *Shakespeare's Blackfriars Playhouse: Its History and Its Design* (New York, 1964) is a detailed study of the Blackfriars, which attempts to establish the details of its physical arrangements.

A sound and readable history of the early theatres is Joseph Quincy Adams, *Shakespearean Playhouses: A History of English Theatres from the Beginnings to the Restoration* (Boston, 1917). For detailed, factual information about the Elizabethan and seventeenth-century stages, the definitive reference works are Sir Edmund Chambers, *The Elizabethan Stage* (4 vols., Oxford, 1923) and Gerald E. Bentley, *The Jacobean and Caroline Stages* (5 vols., Oxford, 1941–1956).

Further information on the history of the theatre and related topics will be found in the following titles: T. W. Baldwin, *The Organization and Personnel of the Shakespearean Company* (Princeton, 1927); Lily Bess Campbell, *Scenes and Machines on the English Stage during the Renaissance* (Cambridge, 1923); Esther Cloudman Dunn, *Shakespeare in America* (New York, 1939); George C. D. Odell, *Shakespeare from Betterton to Irving* (2 vols., London, 1931); Arthur Colby Sprague, *Shakespeare and the Actors: The Stage Business in His Plays (1660–1905)* (Cambridge, Mass., 1944) and *Shakespearian Players and Performances* (Cambridge, Mass., 1953); Leslie Hotson, *The Commonwealth and Restoration Stage* (Cambridge, Mass., 1928); Alwin Thaler, *Shakspere to Sheridan: A Book about the Theatre of Yesterday and To-day* (Cambridge, Mass., 1922); George C. Branam, *Eighteenth-Century Adaptations of Shakespeare's Tragedies* (Berkeley, 1956); C. Beecher Hogan, *Shakespeare in the Theatre, 1701–1800* (Oxford, 1957); Ernest Bradlee Watson, *Sheridan to Robertson: A Study of the 19th-Century London Stage* (Cambridge, Mass., 1926); and Enid Welsford, *The Court Masque* (Cambridge, Mass., 1927).

A brief account of the growth of Shakespeare's reputation is F. E. Halliday, *The Cult of Shakespeare* (London, 1947). A more detailed discussion is given in Augustus Ralli, *A History of Shakespearian Criticism* (2 vols., Oxford, 1932; New York, 1958). Harley Granville-Barker, *Prefaces to Shakespeare* (5 vols., London, 1927–1948; 2 vols., London, 1958) provides stimulating critical discussion of the plays. An older classic of criticism is Andrew C. Bradley, *Shakespearean Tragedy: Lectures on Hamlet, Othello, King Lear, Macbeth* (London, 1904; paperback, 1955). Sir Edmund Chambers, *Shakespeare: A Survey* (London, 1935; paperback, 1958) contains short, sensible essays on thirty-four of the plays, originally written as introductions to single-play editions.

Troilus and Cressida has produced a large literature of discussion and interpretation. An appraisal of scholarship on the play, as well as much sensible interpretation, will be found in Robert Kimbrough, *Shakespeare's Troilus and Cressida and Its Setting* (Cambridge, Mass., 1964). Mr. Kimbrough's bibliography will provide a list of the most valuable studies of the play. A work of great value in appraising the play in its contemporary setting is Oscar J. Campbell, *Comicall Satyre and Shakespeare's Troilus and Cressida* (San Marino, Calif., 1938). A valuable source study is Robert K. Presson, *Shakespeare's Troilus and Cressida and the Legends of Troy* (Madison, Wis., 1953). W. W. Lawrence, in *Shakespeare's Problem Comedies* (New York, 1931), gives a lucid and sensible analysis of the textual problem and a convincing interpretation of the play's content. Versions of the story of Troilus and Cressida as told by Chaucer, Benoît de Saint-More, Boccaccio, and Robert Henryson are collected in *The Story of Troilus*, with translations by R. K. Gordon (Dutton paperback: New York, 1964).

For the history plays see Lily Bess Campbell, *Shakespeare's "Histories": Mirrors of Elizabethan*

Policy (Cambridge, 1947); John Palmer, *Political Characters of Shakespeare* (London, 1945; 1961); E. M. W. Tillyard, *Shakespeare's History Plays* (London, 1948); Irving Ribner, *The English History Play in the Age of Shakespeare* (Princeton, 1947); and Max M. Reese, *The Cease of Majesty* (London, 1961).

The comedies are illuminated by the following studies: C. L. Barber, *Shakespeare's Festive Comedy* (Princeton, 1959); John Russell Brown, *Shakespeare and His Comedies* (London, 1957); H. B. Charlton, *Shakespearian Comedy* (London, 1938; 4th ed., 1949); W. W. Lawrence, *Shakespeare's Problem Comedies* (New York, 1931); and Thomas M. Parrott, *Shakespearean Comedy* (New York, 1949).

Further discussions of Shakespeare's tragedies in addition to Bradley, already cited, are contained in H. B. Charlton, *Shakespearian Tragedy* (Cambridge, 1948); Willard Farnham, *The Medieval Heritage of Elizabethan Tragedy* (Berkeley, 1936) and *Shakespeare's Tragic Frontier: The World of His Final Tragedies* (Berkeley, 1950); and Harold S. Wilson, *On the Design of Shakespearian Tragedy* (Toronto, 1957).

The "Roman" plays are treated in M. M. MacCallum, *Shakespeare's Roman Plays and Their Background* (London, 1910); J. C. Maxwell, "Shakespeare's Roman Plays, 1900–1956," *Shakespeare Survey 10* (Cambridge, 1957), 1-11; Maurice M. Charney, *Shakespeare's Roman Plays: The Function of Imagery in the Drama* (Cambridge, Mass., 1961) and *Discussions of Shakespeare's Roman Plays* (paperback; Boston, 1964).

Kenneth Muir, *Shakespeare's Sources: Comedies and Tragedies* (London, 1957) discusses Shakespeare's use of source material. The sources themselves have been reprinted several times. Among old editions are John P. Collier (ed.), *Shakespeare's Library* (2 vols., London, 1850), Israel C. Gollancz (ed.), *The Shakespeare Classics* (12 vols., London, 1907–1926), and W. C. Hazlitt (ed.), *Shakespeare's Library* (6 vols., London, 1875). A modern edition is being prepared by Geoffrey Bullough with the title *Narrative and Dramatic Sources of Shakespeare* (London and New York, 1957–). Five volumes, covering the sources for the comedies, histories, and Roman plays, have been published to date (1966).

In addition to the second edition of *Webster's New International Dictionary*, which contains most of the unusual words used by Shakespeare, the following reference works are helpful: Edwin A. Abbott, *A Shakespearian Grammar* (London, 1872); C. T. Onions, *A Shakespeare Glossary* (2nd rev. ed., Oxford, 1925); and Eric Partridge, *Shakespeare's Bawdy* (New York, 1948; paperback, 1960).

Some knowledge of the social background of the period in which Shakespeare lived is important for a full understanding of his work. A brief, clear, and accurate account of Tudor history is S. T. Bindoff, *The Tudors*, in the Penguin series. A readable general history is G. M. Trevelyan, *The History of England*, first published in 1926 and available in numerous editions. The same author's *English Social History*, first published in 1942 and also available in many editions, provides fascinating information about England in all periods. Sir John Neale, *Queen Elizabeth* (London, 1935; paperback, 1957) is the best study of the great Queen. Various aspects of life in the Elizabethan period are treated in Louis B. Wright, *Middle-Class Culture in Elizabethan England* (Chapel Hill, N.C., 1935; reprinted Ithaca, N.Y., 1958, 1964). *Shakespeare's England: An Account of the Life and Manners of His Age,* edited by Sidney Lee and C. T. Onions (2 vols., Oxford, 1917), provides much information on many aspects of Elizabethan life. A fascinating survey of the period will be found in Muriel St. C. Byrne, *Elizabethan Life in Town and Country* (London, 1925; rev. ed., 1954; paperback, 1961).

The Folger Library is issuing a series of illustrated booklets entitled "Folger Booklets on Tudor and Stuart Civilization," printed and distributed by Cornell University Press. Published to date are the following titles:

D. W. Davies, *Dutch Influences on English Culture, 1558–1625*

Giles E. Dawson, *The Life of William Shakespeare*

Ellen C. Eyler, *Early English Gardens and Garden Books*

Elaine W. Fowler, *English Sea Power in the Early Tudor Period, 1485–1558*

John R. Hale, *The Art of War and Renaissance England*

William Haller, *Elizabeth I and the Puritans*

Virginia A. LaMar, *English Dress in the Age of Shakespeare*

————, *Travel and Roads in England*

John L. Lievsay, *The Elizabethan Image of Italy*

James G. McManaway, *The Authorship of Shakespeare*

Dorothy E. Mason, *Music in Elizabethan England*

Garrett Mattingly, *The "Invincible" Armada and Elizabethan England*

Boies Penrose, *Tudor and Early Stuart Voyaging*

Conyers Read, *The Government of England under Elizabeth*

Albert J. Schmidt, *The Yeoman in Tudor and Stuart England*

Lilly C. Stone, *English Sports and Recreations*

Craig R. Thompson, *The Bible in English, 1525–1611*

——, *The English Church in the Sixteenth Century*

——, *Schools in Tudor England*

——, *Universities in Tudor England*

Louis B. Wright, *Shakespeare's Theatre and the Dramatic Tradition*

At intervals the Folger Library plans to gather these booklets in hardbound volumes. The first is *Life and Letters in Tudor and Stuart England, First Folger Series,* edited by Louis B. Wright and Virginia A. LaMar (published for the Folger Shakespeare Library by Cornell University Press, 1962). The volume contains eleven of the separate booklets.

Priam, King of Troy.

Hector,
Troilus,
Paris, } his sons.
Deiphobus,
Helenus,
Margarelon, a bastard son of *Priam.*

Aeneas, } Trojan commanders.
Antenor,

Calchas, a Trojan priest, taking part with the Greeks.
Pandarus, uncle to *Cressida.*
Agamemnon, the Grecian General.
Menelaus, his brother.

Achilles,
Ajax,
Ulysses,
Nestor, } Grecian commanders.
Diomedes,
Patroclus,

Thersites, a deformed and scurrilous Grecian.
Alexander, servant to *Cressida.*
Myrmidons, Achaean followers of *Achilles.*
Servant to Troilus.
Servant to Paris.
Servant to Diomedes.

Helen, wife to *Menelaus.*
Andromache, wife to *Hector.*
Cassandra, daughter to *Priam,* a prophetess.
Cressida, daughter to *Calchas.*
Trojan and Greek soldiers and attendants.
      SCENE: *Troy and the Grecian Camp.*]

Pro. The Prologue tells how the Greek siege of Troy resulted from Prince Paris' abduction of Helen, wife of King Menelaus.

2. **orgulous:** haughty (French *orgueilleux*).

4. **Fraught:** laden; **ministers:** agents.

6. **crownets:** coronets.

8. **immures:** walls.

11. **Tenedos:** an island in the Aegean off the coast of Asia Minor near the site of Troy.

13. **Dardan plains:** the cities of Dardania, Troy, and Ilion were joined to form the city known as Troy, Ilion, or Ilium.

15. **brave pavilions:** splendid tents.

17. **massy:** massive.

18. **corresponsive and fulfilling bolts:** bolts corresponding to the staples in size and completely filling them.

19. **Sperr up:** lock in.

THE PROLOGUE

In Troy there lies the scene. From isles of Greece
The princes orgulous, their high blood chafed,
Have to the port of Athens sent their ships,
Fraught with the ministers and instruments
Of cruel war. Sixty and nine, that wore   5
Their crownets regal, from the Athenian bay
Put forth toward Phrygia, and their vow is made
To ransack Troy, within whose strong immures
The ravished Helen, Menelaus' queen,
With wanton Paris sleeps; and that's the quarrel.   10
To Tenedos they come;
And the deep-drawing barks do there disgorge
Their warlike fraughtage. Now on Dardan plains
The fresh and yet unbruised Greeks do pitch
Their brave pavilions. Priam's six-gated city,   15
Dardan, and Timbria, Helias, Chetas, Troien,
And Antenorides with massy staples
And corresponsive and fulfilling bolts
Sperr up the sons of Troy.
Now expectation, tickling skittish spirits,   20
On one and other side, Trojan and Greek,
Sets all on hazard. And hither am I come
A Prologue armed, but not in confidence

I

24. **suited:** clothed.

25. **like conditions:** similar fashion; **argument:** theme.

27. **vaunt and firstlings:** vanguard and firstborn; i.e., initial events.

Asia Minor in the vicinity of Troy. *B* at upper right is the island of Tenedos; *C* inland on the left marks Troy itself. From George Sandys, *A Relation of a Journey* (1627).

Of author's pen or actor's voice, but suited
In like conditions as our argument,   25
To tell you, fair beholders, that our play
Leaps o'er the vaunt and firstlings of those broils,
Beginning in the middle; starting thence away
To what may be digested in a play.
Like, or find fault; do as your pleasures are: 30
Now, good or bad, 'tis but the chance of war.

[Exit.]

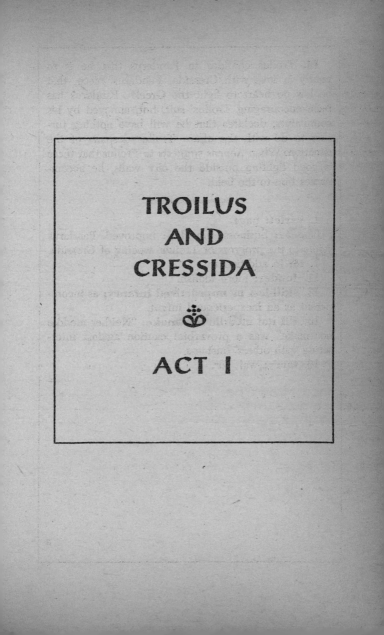

TROILUS
AND
CRESSIDA

ACT I

I.i. Troilus confides to Pandarus that he is so madly in love with Cressida, Pandarus' niece, that he has no heart to fight the Greeks. Pandarus has been encouraging Troilus' suit, but, annoyed by his complaints, declares that he will have nothing further to do with the affair. Troilus despairs of the situation. When Aeneas suggests to Troilus that there is good fighting outside the city walls, he accompanies him to the field.

1. **varlet:** page.

6. **gear:** business; **mended:** improved. Pandarus refers to the progress of Troilus' wooing of Cressida.

7. **to:** in addition to.

11. **fonder:** more foolish.

13. **skill-less as unpracticed infancy:** as incompetent as an inexperienced infant.

15. **I'll not meddle nor make:** "Neither meddle nor make" was a proverbial caution against interfering with others' business.

16. **tarry:** wait for.

ACT I

Scene I. [Troy. Before Priam's Palace.]

Enter Pandarus and Troilus.

Tro. Call here my varlet; I'll unarm again.
Why should I war without the walls of Troy
That find such cruel battle here within?
Each Trojan that is master of his heart,
Let him to field: Troilus, alas, hath none! 5
   Pan. Will this gear ne'er be mended?
   Tro. The Greeks are strong and skillful to their
      strength,
Fierce to their skill and to their fierceness valiant,
But I am weaker than a woman's tear, 10
Tamer than sleep, fonder than ignorance,
Less valiant than the virgin in the night,
And skill-less as unpracticed infancy.
   Pan. Well, I have told you enough of this. For my
part, I'll not meddle nor make no farther. He that will 15
have a cake out of the wheat must needs tarry the
grinding.
   Tro. Have I not tarried?
   Pan. Ay, the grinding; but you must tarry the bolt-
ing. 20

3

22. **bolting:** sifting.

31. **blench:** flinch; **suff'rance:** endurance.

34. **traitor:** addressed to himself for the suggestion that Cressida is not constantly in his mind.

42. **couched:** hidden.

44. **And:** if.

45. **go to:** never mind; I won't dwell on that.

Greeks attacking the walls of Troy. From Isaac de la Rivière, *Speculum heroici* (1613).

Tro. Have I not tarried?

Pan. Ay, the bolting; but you must tarry the leavening.

Tro. Still have I tarried.

Pan. Ay, to the leavening; but here's yet in the 25
word "hereafter" the kneading, the making of the
cake, the heating of the oven, and the baking: nay,
you must stay the cooling too, or you may chance to
burn your lips.

Tro. Patience herself, what goddess e'er she be, 30
Doth lesser blench at suff'rance than I do.
At Priam's royal table do I sit;
And when fair Cressid comes into my thoughts—
So, traitor, then she comes, when is she thence?

Pan. Well, she looked yesternight fairer than ever 35
I saw her look, or any woman else.

Tro. I was about to tell thee: when my heart,
As wedged with a sigh, would rive in twain,
Lest Hector or my father should perceive me,
I have, as when the sun doth light a storm, 40
Buried this sigh in wrinkle of a smile.
But sorrow, that is couched in seeming gladness,
Is like that mirth fate turns to sudden sadness.

Pan. And her hair were not somewhat darker than
Helen's—well, go to—there were no more comparison 45
between the women. But, for my part, she is my kins-
woman: I would not, as they term it, praise her. But
I would somebody had heard her talk yesterday, as I
did. I will not dispraise your sister Cassandra's wit,
but— 50

Tro. O Pandarus! I tell thee, Pandarus—

60. to: in comparison with; **seizure:** touch.

61. cygnet's: young swan's; **spirit of sense:** the most delicate perception of the senses.

71. mends: amends; means of improvement.

73. my labor for my travail: proverbial. **Travail** means "pains."

80. on Friday: i.e., in everyday apparel, as compared with Sunday finery.

When I do tell thee there my hopes lie drowned,
Reply not in how many fathoms deep
They lie endrenched. I tell thee, I am mad
In Cressid's love. Thou answerst, "She is fair"; 55
Pourst in the open ulcer of my heart
Her eyes, her hair, her cheek, her gait, her voice;
Handlest in thy discourse, oh, that her hand,
In whose comparison all whites are ink
Writing their own reproach, to whose soft seizure 60
The cygnet's down is harsh and spirit of sense
Hard as the palm of plowman. This thou tellst me,
As true thou tellst me, when I say I love her;
But, saying thus, instead of oil and balm,
Thou layst in every gash that love hath given me 65
The knife that made it.

   Pan. I speak no more than truth.

   Tro. Thou dost not speak so much.

   Pan. Faith, I'll not meddle in't. Let her be as she is.
If she be fair, 'tis the better for her: and she be not, 70
she has the mends in her own hands.

   Tro. Good Pandarus; how now, Pandarus!

   Pan. I have had my labor for my travail, ill-thought-
on of her, and ill-thought-on of you; gone between
and between, but small thanks for my labor. 75

   Tro. What, art thou angry, Pandarus? What, with
me?

   Pan. Because she's kin to me, therefore she's not so
fair as Helen: and she were not kin to me, she would
be as fair on Friday as Helen is on Sunday. But what 80
care I? I care not and she were a blackamoor: 'tis all
one to me.

85. her father: as is revealed later in the play, Cressida's father, Calchas, had foreseen the destruction of Troy and joined the Greek side. Cressida, however, remained in Troy.

97. fight upon this argument: accept the controversy over Helen as a reason to fight.

101. tetchy: peevish.

103. Daphne: a nymph who fled from Apollo's advances (Ovid, *Metamorphoses*, bk. i).

104. we: the royal plural; himself.

106. Ilium: apparently meaning specifically the royal palace.

Apollo and Daphne. From Ovid, *Metamorphoses* (1509).

Tro. Say I she is not fair?

Pan. I do not care whether you do or not. She's a
fool to stay behind her father. Let her to the Greeks: 85
and so I'll tell her the next time I see her. For my
part, I'll meddle nor make no more i' the matter.

Tro. Pandarus—

Pan. Not I.

Tro. Sweet Pandarus—   90

Pan. Pray you, speak no more to me. I will leave all
as I found it, and there an end.   *Exit.*

Sound Alarum.

Tro. Peace, you ungracious clamors; peace, rude
    sounds!
Fools on both sides! Helen must needs be fair,   95
When with your blood you daily paint her thus.
I cannot fight upon this argument:
It is too starved a subject for my sword.
But Pandarus—O gods, how do you plague me!
I cannot come to Cressid but by Pandar;   100
And he's as tetchy to be wooed to woo
As she is stubborn-chaste against all suit.
Tell me, Apollo, for thy Daphne's love,
What Cressid is, what Pandar, and what we.
Her bed is India: there she lies, a pearl.   105
Between our Ilium and where she resides,
Let it be called the wild and wand'ring flood,
Ourself the merchant, and this sailing Pandar
Our doubtful hope, our convoy, and our bark.   *Alarum.*

112. **sorts:** is appropriate.

118. **a scar to scorn:** a scar in comparison with the scorn which Menelaus has received as a result of Paris' abduction of Helen.

119. **horn:** the figurative horns that the betrayed husband was said to have.

121. **if "would I might" were "may":** that is, if he, Troilus, could have his wish concerning Cressida.

━━━━━━━━━━━━━━━━━━━━━━━━━━━━━━━━━━━━

I. [ii.] Alexander, servant to Cressida, reports to her that Hector has been angered by a defeat at the hands of Ajax (his cousin, but a member of the Greek forces). Ajax is such a combination of folly and vanity that Hector feels disgraced at the defeat. When Pandarus appears, Cressida baits him by speaking slightingly of Troilus in comparison with the other Trojan heroes, who pass in review. Pandarus praises Troilus' martial prowess and handsome person, while Cressida pretends to be unimpressed. Alone, however, she reveals that Troilus has already won her heart. She is reluctant to exchange her advantage as a woman being wooed for that of a woman conquered and determines to keep him ignorant of her true feelings.

Enter Aeneas.

Aen. How now, Prince Troilus! wherefore not 110
    afield?
Tro. Because not there. This woman's answer sorts,
For womanish it is to be from thence.
What news, Aeneas, from the field today?
Aen. That Paris is returned home, and hurt.   115
Tro. By whom, Aeneas?
Aen.   Troilus, by Menelaus.
Tro. Let Paris bleed. 'Tis but a scar to scorn:
Paris is gored with Menelaus' horn.   *Alarum.*
Aen. Hark what good sport is out of town today! 120
Tro. Better at home, if "would I might" were "may."
But to the sport abroad! Are you bound thither?
Aen. In all swift haste.
Tro.   Come, go we then together.
                          Exeunt.

[Scene II. The same. A street.]

Enter Cressida and [Alexander,] her man.

Cres. Who were those went by?
Alex.   Queen Hecuba and Helen.
Cres. And whither go they?
Alex.   Up to the eastern tower,
Whose height commands as subject all the vale,   5
To see the battle. Hector, whose patience

7. **moved:** angry.

9. **like as:** as if; **husbandry:** thrifty management (of time, in this instance). Like a prudent farmer, Hector has arisen early to attend to affairs.

15. **noise:** rumor.

17. **nephew to Hector:** Shakespeare seems to have thought that Ajax was Telamon's son by Priam's sister, Hesione, although Periboea, or Eriboea, of Megara, is recorded as his actual mother. The error was to be found in one of his sources, Caxton's *Recuyell of . . . Troy,* and was currently accepted in his age. See also [IV. v.] 96 and 136-37.

20. **per se:** by himself; i.e., incomparable.

25. **particular additions:** personal distinguishing epithets.

27. **humors:** body fluids supposed to determine temperament.

30. **glimpse:** touch; **attaint:** fault; blemish.

32. **against the hair:** unnaturally; perversely.

34. **Briareus:** one of the Titans of Greek mythology, possessed of a hundred hands; **purblind:** totally blind; **Argus:** the monster of a hundred eyes in Greek mythology.

Is as a virtue fixed, today was moved.
He chid Andromache and struck his armorer;
And, like as there were husbandry in war,
Before the sun rose he was harnessed light,   10
And to the field goes he; where every flower
Did, as a prophet, weep what it foresaw
In Hector's wrath.

    Cres.   What was his cause of anger?

    Alex. The noise goes, this: there is among the   15
    Greeks
A lord of Trojan blood, nephew to Hector:
They call him Ajax.

    Cres.   Good: and what of him?

    Alex. They say he is a very man *per se*,   20
And stands alone.

    Cres. So do all men, unless they are drunk, sick, or
have no legs.

    Alex. This man, lady, hath robbed many beasts of
their particular additions. He is as valiant as the lion,   25
churlish as the bear, slow as the elephant: a man into
whom nature hath so crowded humors that his valor
is crushed into folly, his folly sauced with discretion.
There is no man hath a virtue that he hath not a
glimpse of, nor any man an attaint but he carries   30
some stain of it. He is melancholy without cause and
merry against the hair. He hath the joints of everything, but everything so out of joint that he is a gouty
Briareus, many hands and no use, or purblind Argus,
all eyes and no sight.   35

    Cres. But how should this man, that makes me
smile, make Hector angry?

38. coped: matched himself against.

41. waking: sleepless.

49-50. cousin: a general term of address between near relations or to express affable familiarity.

Hector and Ajax. From Lodovico Dolce, *Le transformationi* (1570).

9

Alex. They say he yesterday coped Hector in the
battle and struck him down, the disdain and shame
whereof hath ever since kept Hector fasting and   40
waking.

Enter Pandarus.

Cres. Who comes here?

Alex. Madam, your uncle Pandarus.

Cres. Hector's a gallant man.

Alex. As may be in the world, lady.   45

Pan. What's that? What's that?

Cres. Good morrow, uncle Pandarus.

Pan. Good morrow, cousin Cressid. What do you
talk of? Good morrow, Alexander. How do you, cousin? When were you at Ilium?   50

Cres. This morning, uncle.

Pan. What were you talking of when I came? Was
Hector armed and gone ere you came to Ilium? Helen
was not up, was she?

Cres. Hector was gone, but Helen was not up.   55

Pan. E'en so: Hector was stirring early.

Cres. That were we talking of, and of his anger.

Pan. Was he angry?

Cres. So he says here.

Pan. True, he was so: I know the cause too. He'll   60
lay about him today, I can tell them that. And there's
Troilus will not come far behind him. Let them take
heed of Troilus, I can tell them that too.

Cres. What, is he angry too?

74. **in some degrees:** by many degrees.

78. **Condition:** i.e., I would he were himself, if I had to go barefoot to India to make it possible.

80. **'a:** he.

87. **come to't:** arrived at maturity.

89. **wit:** intelligence; **this year:** for a long time to come.

Pan. Who, Troilus? Troilus is the better man of the   65
two.

Cres. O Jupiter! there's no comparison.

Pan. What, not between Troilus and Hector? Do
you know a man if you see him?

Cres. Ay, if I ever saw him before and knew him.   70

Pan. Well, I say Troilus is Troilus.

Cres. Then you say as I say; for I am sure he is not
Hector.

Pan. No, nor Hector is not Troilus in some degrees.

Cres. 'Tis just to each of them: he is himself.   75

Pan. Himself! Alas, poor Troilus! I would he were.

Cres. So he is.

Pan. Condition I had gone barefoot to India.

Cres. He is not Hector.

Pan. Himself! no, he's not himself. Would 'a were   80
himself! Well, the gods are above: time must friend
or end. Well, Troilus, well, I would my heart were in
her body! No, Hector is not a better man than Troilus.

Cres. Excuse me.

Pan. He is elder.   85

Cres. Pardon me, pardon me.

Pan. The other's not come to't: you shall tell me
another tale, when the other's come to't. Hector shall
not have his wit this year.

Cres. He shall not need it, if he have his own.   90

Pan. Nor his qualities.

Cres. No matter.

Pan. Nor his beauty.

Cres. 'Twould not become him: his own's better.

Pan. You have no judgment, niece. Helen herself   95

96. **favor:** appearance; complexion.

104. **should:** must.

112. **merry Greek:** roisterer; wanton.

114. **compassed:** round.

116. **tapster's arithmetic:** it was traditional to make fun of the poor head for figures attributed to tavern keepers and their help.

116-17. **bring his particulars . . . to a total:** add up his personal holdings.

120. **old:** experienced; **lifter:** slang for "thief."

122. **puts me:** puts (the ethical dative construction, indicating the speaker's interest in the action).

swore the other day that Troilus, for a brown favor—
for so 'tis, I must confess—not brown neither—

Cres. No, but brown.

Pan. Faith, to say truth, brown and not brown.

Cres. To say the truth, true and not true.   100

Pan. She praised his complexion above Paris.

Cres. Why, Paris hath color enough.

Pan. So he has.

Cres. Then Troilus should have too much. If she
praised him above, his complexion is higher than his: 105
he having color enough, and the other higher, is too
flaming a praise for a good complexion. I had as lief
Helen's golden tongue had commended Troilus for a
copper nose.

Pan. I swear to you, I think Helen loves him better 110
than Paris.

Cres. Then she's a merry Greek indeed.

Pan. Nay, I am sure she does. She came to him the
other day into the compassed window—and, you
know, he has not past three or four hairs on his chin— 115

Cres. Indeed, a tapster's arithmetic may soon bring
his particulars therein to a total.

Pan. Why, he is very young: and yet will he, within
three pound, lift as much as his brother Hector.

Cres. Is he so young a man and so old a lifter?   120

Pan. But, to prove to you that Helen loves him: she
came and puts me her white hand to his cloven chin—

Cres. Juno have mercy! how came it cloven?

Pan. Why, you know, 'tis dimpled: I think his smil-
ing becomes him better than any man in all Phrygia. 125

Cres. Oh, he smiles valiantly.

128. **and 'twere:** as though it were.

129. **go to:** all right; say no more.

141. **takes upon her:** pretends.

146. **millstones:** "He weeps millstones" was an ironic saying expressing doubt of someone's sincerity.

Pan. Does he not?

Cres. Oh, yes, and 'twere a cloud in autumn.

Pan. Why, go to, then. But to prove to you that Helen loves Troilus— 130

Cres. Troilus will stand to the proof, if you'll prove it so.

Pan. Troilus! why, he esteems her no more than I esteem an addle egg.

Cres. If you love an addle egg as well as you love 135
an idle head, you would eat chickens i' the shell.

Pan. I cannot choose but laugh to think how she tickled his chin; indeed, she has a marvell's white hand, I must needs confess—

Cres. Without the rack. 140

Pan. And she takes upon her to spy a white hair on his chin.

Cres. Alas, poor chin! many a wart is richer.

Pan. But there was such laughing! Queen Hecuba laughed that her eyes ran o'er. 145

Cres. With millstones.

Pan. And Cassandra laughed.

Cres. But there was a more temperate fire under the pot of her eyes: did her eyes run o'er too?

Pan. And Hector laughed. 150

Cres. At what was all this laughing?

Pan. Marry, at the white hair that Helen spied on Troilus' chin.

Cres. And't had been a green hair, I should have laughed too. 155

Pan. They laughed not so much at the hair as at his pretty answer.

166. **forked:** horned; see I. i. 119.
169. **passed:** surpassed; beat everything.
178. **against:** at the beginning of.
184. **bravely:** splendidly.

Cres. What was his answer?

Pan. Quoth she, "Here's but two-and-fifty hairs on
your chin, and one of them is white."   160

Cres. This is her question.

Pan. That's true; make no question of that. "Two-
and-fifty hairs," quoth he, "and one white: that white
hair is my father, and all the rest are his sons."
"Jupiter!" quoth she, "which of these hairs is Paris my 165
husband?" "The forked one," quoth he, "pluck't out
and give it him." But there was such laughing! and
Helen so blushed, and Paris so chafed, and all the rest
so laughed, that it passed.

Cres. So let it now, for it has been a great while 170
going by.

Pan. Well, cousin, I told you a thing yesterday:
think on't.

Cres. So I do.

Pan. I'll be sworn 'tis true: he will weep you, an 175
'twere a man born in April.

Cres. And I'll spring up in his tears, an 'twere a
nettle against May.   *Sound a retreat.*

Pan. Hark! they are coming from the field. Shall we
stand up here and see them as they pass toward 180
Ilium? Good niece, do, sweet niece Cressida.

Cres. At your pleasure.

Pan. Here, here, here's an excellent place: here we
may see most bravely. I'll tell you them all by their
names as they pass by; but mark Troilus above the 185
rest.

188. **brave:** gallant.

192. **shrewd:** sharp.

194. **whosoever:** in comparison with anyone.

194-95. **proper man of person:** man of handsome person.

198. **give you the nod:** Cressida implies that Pandarus is a "noddy," (fool), therefore, to give him the **nod** would mean giving him additional foolishness or the title "fool" that he already possesses.

200. **the rich shall have more:** i.e., Troilus' action will be superfluous.

Aeneas [passes].

Cres. Speak not so loud.
Pan. That's Aeneas. Is not that a brave man? He's
one of the flowers of Troy, I can tell you. But mark
Troilus: you shall see anon. 190
Cres. Who's that?

Antenor [passes].

Pan. That's Antenor. He has a shrewd wit, I can tell
you; and he's a man good enough. He's one o' the
soundest judgments in Troy, whosoever, and a proper
man of person. When comes Troilus? I'll show you 195
Troilus anon. If he sees me, you shall see him nod at
me.
Cres. Will he give you the nod?
Pan. You shall see.
Cres. If he do, the rich shall have more. 200

Hector [passes].

Pan. That's Hector, that, that, look you, that: there's
a fellow! Go thy way, Hector! There's a brave man,
niece. Oh, brave Hector! Look how he looks! There's
a countenance! Is't not a brave man?
Cres. Oh, a brave man! 205
Pan. Is 'a not? It does a man's heart good. Look you
what hacks are on his helmet! Look you yonder, do
you see? Look you there. There's no jesting: there's

209. **laying on:** evidence of the laying on of blows.

212. **and:** if.

laying on, take't off who will, as they say. There be
hacks!   210

Cres. Be those with swords?

Pan. Swords! anything, he cares not; and the Devil
come to him, it's all one. By God's lid, it does one's
heart good. Yonder comes Paris, yonder comes Paris.

Paris [passes].

Look ye yonder, niece. Is't not a gallant man too, is't   215
not? Why, this is brave now. Who said he came hurt
home today? He's not hurt. Why, this will do Helen's
heart good now, ha! Would I could see Troilus now!
You shall see Troilus anon.

Cres. Who's that?   220

Helenus [passes].

Pan. That's Helenus. I marvel where Troilus is.
That's Helenus. I think he went not forth today.
That's Helenus.

Cres. Can Helenus fight, uncle?

Pan. Helenus! no. Yes, he'll fight indifferent well. I   225
marvel where Troilus is. Hark! do you not hear the
people cry "Troilus"? Helenus is a priest.

Cres. What sneaking fellow comes yonder?

Troilus [passes].

Pan. Where? Yonder? That's Deiphobus. 'Tis

235. **helm:** helmet.
241. **to boot:** in addition.

Agamemnon. From Geoffrey Whitney, *A Choice of Emblems* (1586).

Troilus! There's a man, niece! Hem! Brave Troilus! 230
the prince of chivalry!

Cres. Peace, for shame, peace!

Pan. Mark him: note him. Oh, brave Troilus! Look
well upon him, niece. Look you how his sword is
bloodied and his helm more hacked than Hector's, 235
and how he looks, and how he goes! Oh, admirable
youth! he never saw three-and-twenty. Go thy way,
Troilus, go thy way! Had I a sister were a grace, or a
daughter a goddess, he should take his choice. Oh,
admirable man! Paris? Paris is dirt to him; and, I war- 240
rant, Helen, to change, would give an eye to boot.

Common Soldiers [pass].

Cres. Here comes more.

Pan. Asses, fools, dolts! Chaff and bran, chaff and
bran! Porridge after meat! I could live and die in the
eyes of Troilus. Ne'er look, ne'er look. The eagles are 245
gone. Crows and daws, crows and daws! I had rather
be such a man as Troilus than Agamemnon and all
Greece.

Cres. There is amongst the Greeks Achilles, a better
man than Troilus.   250

Pan. Achilles! A drayman, a porter, a very camel.

Cres. Well, well.

Pan. Well, well! Why, have you any discretion?
Have you any eyes? Do you know what a man is?
Is not birth, beauty, good shape, discourse, manhood, 255
learning, gentleness, virtue, youth, liberality, and
suchlike the spice and salt that season a man?

258. **minced:** pun on "mincing," effeminate.

259. **the man's date is out:** i.e., he is no longer manly. Dates were popular in pie fillings.

260-61. **at what ward you lie:** how to take you; literally, what defense you rely upon.

264. **honesty:** reputation.

266. **watches:** watchposts; vigils.

267. **watches:** causes of wakefulness; lovers.

268. **watch:** have an eye to; be wary of.

269-70. **what I would not have hit:** i.e., her chastity.

270. **watch you for telling:** see to it that you do not tell.

272. **watching:** guarding.

277. **doubt:** fear.

281. **To bring:** the phrase "I will be with you to bring" implied a threat, but Pandarus replies literally.

Cres. Ay, a minced man. And then to be baked with
no date in the pie, for then the man's date is out.

Pan. You are such a woman! A man knows not at 260
what ward you lie.

Cres. Upon my back, to defend my belly; upon my
wit, to defend my wiles; upon my secrecy, to defend
mine honesty; my mask, to defend my beauty; and
you, to defend all these. And at all these wards I lie, 265
at a thousand watches.

Pan. Say one of your watches.

Cres. Nay, I'll watch you for that; and that's one of
the chiefest of them too. If I cannot ward what I
would not have hit, I can watch you for telling how 270
I took the blow; unless it swell past hiding, and then
it's past watching.

Pan. You are such another!

Enter [Troilus'] Boy.

Boy. Sir, my lord would instantly speak with you.
Pan. Where?   275
Boy. At your own house: there he unarms him.
Pan. Good boy, tell him I come. [*Exit Boy.*] I doubt
he be hurt. Fare ye well, good niece.
Cres. Adieu, uncle.
Pan. I will be with you, niece, by and by.   280
Cres. To bring, uncle?
Pan. Ay, a token from Troilus.
Cres. By the same token, you are a bawd.

Exit Pandarus.

Words, vows, gifts, tears, and love's full sacrifice

291. **is:** is worth.

294. **out of love:** derived from the ways of love.

295. **Achievement is command; ungained, beseech:** conquest makes men commanding; before they conquer, they beg for favor.

:::

I. [iii.] Agamemnon holds a council of war. He and Nestor try to hearten the other Greek leaders, depressed at the failure of their seven-year siege of Troy. They point out that adversity is Fortune's test of men's true quality. Ulysses, however, declares that Troy would already have been taken if due attention had been paid to order and degree. Agamemnon's authority has been flouted by Achilles and by his example the whole Greek army has lost respect for authority. Aeneas interrupts with a message from Prince Hector, challenging to single combat any Greek who would maintain the superior virtue and beauty of his mistress over Hector's lady. Although he realizes that the challenge is meant for Achilles, Ulysses craftily suggests that if their most eminent warrior should be defeated by Hector, the morale of the Greek forces would be damaged. If Achilles should win, on the other hand, his pride would be further swelled. Ulysses proposes that they contrive a lottery so that Ajax will draw the winning lot. Whether Ajax wins or loses, his assumption of the role of Greek champion should humble Achilles' pride.

:::

Entrance. **Sennet:** a trumpet call.

8. **his:** its.

9. **Tortive and errant:** so that it becomes twisted and wandering; i.e., distorted.

18

He offers in another's enterprise.   285
But more in Troilus thousandfold I see
Than in the glass of Pandar's praise may be:
Yet hold I off. Women are angels, wooing.
Things won are done; joy's soul lies in the doing.
That she beloved knows naught that knows not this: 290
Men prize the thing ungained more than it is,
That she was never yet that ever knew
Love got so sweet as when desire did sue.
Therefore this maxim out of love I teach:
Achievement is command; ungained, beseech.   295
Then, though my heart's content firm love doth bear,
Nothing of that shall from mine eyes appear.

Exeunt.

[Scene III. The Grecian Camp. Before Agamemnon's tent.]

*Sennet. Enter Agamemnon, Nestor, Ulysses,
Diomedes, Menelaus, with others.*

  Aga. Princes,
What grief hath set the jaundice on your cheeks?
The ample proposition that hope makes
In all designs begun on earth below
Fails in the promised largeness. Checks and disasters   5
Grow in the veins of actions highest reared,
As knots, by the conflux of meeting sap,
Infects the sound pine and diverts his grain
Tortive and errant from his course of growth.

11. **suppose:** expectation.

13. **Sith:** since.

15. **Bias and thwart:** awry.

16. **unbodied figure:** imaginary form.

20. **protractive:** protracted; long-drawn-out.

22. **The fineness of which metal is not found:** that is, the quality of men's metal (mettle) does not appear.

23. **In Fortune's love:** when Fortune is favorable.

24. **artist:** student of arts; scholar.

25. **affined:** related.

28. **light:** chaff; inferior matter.

30. **Lies rich in virtue and unmingled:** is left alone in its full, unadulterated worth.

35. **bauble:** light.

38. **Boreas:** the north wind.

39. **Thetis:** a sea-goddess, mother of Achilles, here personifying the sea.

Boreas abducting the nymph Orithyia. From Gabriele Simeoni, *La vita et Metamorfoseo d'Ovidio* (1559).

Nor, princes, is it matter new to us   10
That we come short of our suppose so far
That after seven years' siege yet Troy walls stand;
Sith every action that hath gone before,
Whereof we have record, trial did draw
Bias and thwart, not answering the aim   15
And that unbodied figure of the thought
That gave't surmised shape. Why then, you princes,
Do you with cheeks abashed behold our works
And call them shames? which are indeed naught else
But the protractive trials of great Jove   20
To find persistive constancy in men.
The fineness of which metal is not found
In Fortune's love; for then the bold and coward,
The wise and fool, the artist and unread,
The hard and soft, seem all affined and kin.   25
But in the wind and tempest of her frown,
Distinction with a broad and powerful fan,
Puffing at all, winnows the light away,
And what hath mass or matter by itself
Lies rich in virtue and unmingled.   30
    Nes. With due observance of thy godlike seat,
Great Agamemnon, Nestor shall apply
Thy latest words. In the reproof of chance
Lies the true proof of men. The sea being smooth,
How many shallow bauble boats dare sail   35
Upon her ancient breast, making their way
With those of nobler bulk!
But let the ruffian Boreas once enrage
The gentle Thetis and anon behold
The strong-ribbed bark through liquid mountains cut,   40

42. **Perseus' horse:** the winged horse Pegasus, which was engendered by the blood of Medusa when Perseus struck off her head.

45. **toast:** tidbit, like the morsels floated in various drinks.

46. **show:** appearance.

47. **her ray and brightness:** the brightness of her ray.

48. **breese:** gadfly.

50. **knotted:** gnarled.

51. **fled:** have fled.

60. **shut up:** confined.

63. **sway:** rule.

64-5. **stretched-out:** lengthy.

69. **hatched in silver:** having hair streaked with silver. Hatched is a term from heraldry.

70. **air:** breath; words.

The image of the orator whose words "knit" the ears of his listeners to his tongue is illustrated in this picture of the Gallic Hercules, who was famed for his eloquence. From Vincenzo Cartari, *Imagini de gli dei delli antichi* (1615). 20

Bounding between the two moist elements,
Like Perseus' horse. Where's then the saucy boat,
Whose weak untimbered sides but even now
Corrivaled greatness? Either to harbor fled,
Or made a toast for Neptune. Even so   45
Doth valor's show and valor's worth divide
In storms of Fortune. For in her ray and brightness
The herd hath more annoyance by the breese
Than by the tiger; but when the splitting wind
Makes flexible the knees of knotted oaks,   50
And flies fled under shade, why then the thing of
     courage,
As roused with rage, with rage doth sympathize,
And with an accent tuned in selfsame key
Retorts to chiding Fortune.   55
     Uly.   Agamemnon,
Thou great commander, nerve and bone of Greece,
Heart of our numbers, soul and only spirit,
In whom the tempers and the minds of all
Should be shut up, hear what Ulysses speaks.   60
Besides the applause and approbation
The which, [*To Agamemnon*] most mighty for thy
     place and sway,
[*To Nestor*] And thou most reverend for thy stretched-
     out life,   65
I give to both your speeches, which were such
As Agamemnon and the hand of Greece
Should hold up high in brass, and such again
As venerable Nestor, hatched in silver,
Should with a bond of air, strong as the axletree   70
On which the Heavens ride, knit all the Greekish ears

74. **of less expect:** no more expected.

75. **importless burden:** unimportant weight.

77. **mastic:** scourging; vituperative.

79. **his basis:** its foundation.

81. **instances:** items to be enumerated.

82. **specialty:** special restriction to the proper persons.

83. **look how many:** however many.

85. **When that:** when.

87. **vizarded:** masked; obscured.

88. **shows:** appears; **mask:** masked performance.

89. **this center:** the earth, the central point of the cosmos.

91. **Insisture:** permanency of station or place.

95. **med'cinable:** medicinal; remedial.

96. **ill aspects:** malevolent influences.

97. **posts:** speeds.

100. **mutiny:** uproar.

Ulysses. From Guillaume Rouillé, *Promptuarii iconum* (1553).

To his experienced tongue, yet let it please both,
Thou great and wise, to hear Ulysses speak.

   Aga. Speak, Prince of Ithaca; and be't of less expect
That matter needless, of importless burden,   75
Divide thy lips than we are confident,
When rank Thersites opes his mastic jaws,
We shall hear music, wit, and oracle.

   Uly. Troy, yet upon his basis, had been down,
And the great Hector's sword had lacked a master,   80
But for these instances.
The specialty of rule hath been neglected:
And, look how many Grecian tents do stand
Hollow upon this plain, so many hollow factions.
When that the general is not like the hive   85
To whom the foragers shall all repair,
What honey is expected? Degree being vizarded,
The unworthiest shows as fairly in the mask.
The Heavens themselves, the planets, and this center,
Observe degree, priority, and place,   90
Insisture, course, proportion, season, form,
Office, and custom, in all line of order:
And therefore is the glorious planet Sol
In noble eminence enthroned and sphered
Amidst the other; whose med'cinable eye   95
Corrects the ill aspects of planets evil,
And posts like the commandment of a king,
Sans check, to good and bad. But when the planets
In evil mixture to disorder wander,
What plagues and what portents, what mutiny,   100
What raging of the sea, shaking of earth,
Commotion in the winds, frights, changes, horrors,

103. **deracinate:** uproot.

109. **dividable:** dividing; separate.

110. **primogenity and due of birth:** the first-born's right of inheritance.

114. **meets:** confronts.

115. **mere oppugnancy:** downright opposition; **bounded:** limited; kept within bounds.

118. **imbecility:** feebleness (of body rather than mind).

121. **jar:** conflict.

123. **includes itself:** is limited by; resolves itself.

129. **suffocate:** suffocated.

Chaos, "when fire, and air, and earth, and water all were one," as Whitney describes it. From Geoffrey Whitney, *A Choice of Emblems* (1586).

Divert and crack, rend and deracinate
The unity and married calm of states
Quite from their fixure! Oh, when degree is shaked,   105
Which is the ladder to all high designs,
The enterprise is sick! How could communities,
Degrees in schools and brotherhoods in cities,
Peaceful commerce from dividable shores,
The primogenity and due of birth,   110
Prerogative of age, crowns, scepters, laurels,
But by degree, stand in authentic place?
Take but degree away, untune that string,
And hark what discord follows. Each thing meets
In mere oppugnancy. The bounded waters   115
Should lift their bosoms higher than the shores
And make a sop of all this solid globe;
Strength should be lord of imbecility,
And the rude son should strike his father dead;
Force should be right, or rather, right and wrong,   120
Between whose endless jar justice resides,
Should lose their names, and so should justice too.
Then everything includes itself in power,
Power into will, will into appetite;
And appetite, an universal wolf,   125
So doubly seconded with will and power,
Must make perforce an universal prey,
And last eat up himself. Great Agamemnon,
This chaos, when degree is suffocate,
Follows the choking.   130
And this neglection of degree it is
That by a pace goes backward, with a purpose
It hath to climb. The general's disdained

140. **sinews:** strength.

142. **discovered:** revealed.

151. **Upon a lazy bed:** i.e., lazily upon a bed.

155. **pageants:** enacts; makes a show of.

156. **topless:** untoppable; supreme; **deputation:** authority.

157. **conceit:** imagination; skill.

158. **hamstring:** haunch; i.e., vigorous stride.

159-60. **the wooden dialogue and sound/ 'Twixt his stretched footing and the scaffoldage:** the sound of his exaggerated stride echo from the theatre's wooden structure.

161. **o'erwrested seeming:** distorted simulation.

163. **a-mending:** being tuned; **unsquared:** unfitting.

164. **Typhon:** a monster with one hundred heads and a terrifying voice.

By him one step below; he by the next;
That next by him beneath: so every step,   135
Exampled by the first pace that is sick
Of his superior, grows to an envious fever
Of pale and bloodless emulation.
And 'tis this fever that keeps Troy on foot,
Not her own sinews. To end a tale of length,   140
Troy in our weakness stands, not in her strength.

   Nes. Most wisely hath Ulysses here discovered
The fever whereof all our power is sick.

   Aga. The nature of the sickness found, Ulysses,
What is the remedy?   145

   Uly. The great Achilles, whom opinion crowns
The sinew and the forehand of our host,
Having his ear full of his airy fame,
Grows dainty of his worth and in his tent
Lies mocking our designs. With him Patroclus,   150
Upon a lazy bed, the livelong day
Breaks scurril jests;
And with ridiculous and silly action,
Which, slanderer, he imitation calls,
He pageants us. Sometime, great Agamemnon,   155
Thy topless deputation he puts on;
And, like a strutting player—whose conceit
Lies in his hamstring, and doth think it rich
To hear the wooden dialogue and sound
'Twixt his stretched footing and the scaffoldage—   160
Such to-be-pitied and o'erwrested seeming
He acts thy greatness in: and when he speaks,
'Tis like a chime a-mending, with terms unsquared,
Which, from the tongue of roaring Typhon dropped,

165. **Would seem hyperboles:** i.e., his rant would seem exaggerated even for the roaring Typhon; **fusty:** stale.

168. **just:** exactly.

170. **dressed to:** prepared for.

172. **Vulcan:** an ugly cripple, whose wife was Venus, the goddess of beauty.

174. **me:** for me.

178. **gorget:** armor piece for the throat.

182. **spleen:** the organ responsible for fits of anger and laughter.

184. **Severals and generals of grace:** graces that characterize them individually and generally.

188. **paradoxes:** absurdities.

192-93. **bears his head/ In such a rein:** behaves as proudly.

194. **broad:** unrestrained; **keeps:** keeps to.

195. **Makes factious feasts:** arranges feasts for his followers; **state of war:** war council.

Would seem hyperboles. At this fusty stuff,   165
The large Achilles, on his pressed bed lolling,
From his deep chest laughs out a loud applause,
Cries, "Excellent! 'tis Agamemnon just.
Now play me Nestor: hem and stroke thy beard
As he, being dressed to some oration."   170
That's done, as near as the extremest ends
Of parallels, as like as Vulcan and his wife.
Yet god Achilles still cries, "Excellent!
'Tis Nestor right. Now play him me, Patroclus,
Arming to answer in a night alarm."   175
And then, forsooth, the faint defects of age
Must be the scene of mirth; to cough and spit,
And, with a palsy fumbling on his gorget,
Shake in and out the rivet. And at this sport
Sir Valor dies, cries, "Oh, enough, Patroclus,   180
Or give me ribs of steel! I shall split all
In pleasure of my spleen." And in this fashion
All our abilities, gifts, natures, shapes,
Severals and generals of grace exact,
Achievements, plots, orders, preventions,   185
Excitements to the field or speech for truce,
Success or loss, what is or is not, serves
As stuff for these two to make paradoxes.
  Nes. And in the imitation of these twain,
Who, as Ulysses says, opinion crowns   190
With an imperial voice, many are infect.
Ajax is grown self-willed and bears his head
In such a rein, in full as proud a place
As broad Achilles; keeps his tent like him;
Makes factious feasts; rails on our state of war   195

199. **our exposure:** our exposed selves.

200. **rank:** plentifully.

201. **tax:** criticize; **policy:** prudence.

203. **Forestall prescience:** obstruct foresight.

209. **mapp'ry:** mapmaking; i.e., contemptible bookish warfare; **closet:** boudoir; chamber.

211. **swinge:** force.

216. **Makes:** amounts to; is worth.

Roman soldiers with a battering ram. From Guillaume Du Choul, *Discours . . . de la castramentation* (1581).

25

Bold as an oracle, and sets Thersites,
A slave whose gall coins slanders like a mint,
To match us in comparisons with dirt,
To weaken and discredit our exposure,
How rank soever rounded in with danger.   200

   Uly. They tax our policy and call it cowardice,
Count wisdom as no member of the war,
Forestall prescience and esteem no act
But that of hand. The still and mental parts,
That do contrive how many hands shall strike   205
When fitness calls them on and know by measure
Of their observant toil the enemies' weight—
Why, this hath not a finger's dignity!
They call this bed work, mapp'ry, closet war;
So that the ram that batters down the wall,   210
For the great swinge and rudeness of his poise,
They place before his hand that made the engine,
Or those that with the fineness of their souls
By reason guide his execution.

   Nes. Let this be granted and Achilles' horse   215
Makes many Thetis' sons.   *Tucket.*
   Aga. What trumpet? Look, Menelaus.
   Men. From Troy.

Enter Aeneas.

   Aga. What would you 'fore our tent?
   Aen. Is this great Agamemnon's tent, I pray you? 220
   Aga. Even this.
   Aen. May one that is a herald and a prince
Do a fair message to his kingly ears?

235. **youthful Phoebus:** early sun.

240. **free:** frank; generous; **debonair:** gracious.

241. **fame:** reputation.

242. **galls:** capacity for anger; valor.

243-44. **Jove's accord:** "God willing," as a modern would say.

245. **Nothing so full of heart:** no one is braver.

247. **distains:** mars.

250. **sole:** solely.

Aeneas. From Guillaume Rouillé, *Promptuarii iconum* (1553).

   Aga. With surety stronger than Achilles' arm
'Fore all the Greekish heads, which with one voice   225
Call Agamemnon head and general.
   Aen. Fair leave and large security. How may
A stranger to those most imperial looks
Know them from eyes of other mortals?
   Aga.   How!   230
   Aen. Ay.
I ask, that I might waken reverence
And bid the cheek be ready with a blush
Modest as morning when she coldly eyes
The youthful Phoebus.   235
Which is that god in office, guiding men?
Which is the high and mighty Agamemnon?
   Aga. This Trojan scorns us, or the men of Troy
Are ceremonious courtiers.
   Aen. Courtiers as free, as debonair, unarmed,   240
As bending angels: that's their fame in peace.
But when they would seem soldiers, they have galls,
Good arms, strong joints, true swords; and, Jove's accord,
Nothing so full of heart. But peace, Aeneas!   245
Peace, Trojan! Lay thy finger on thy lips!
The worthiness of praise distains his worth,
If that the praised himself bring the praise forth:
But what the repining enemy commends,
That breath Fame blows; that praise, sole pure, tran-   250
   scends.
   Aga. Sir, you of Troy, call you yourself Aeneas?
   Aen. Ay, Greek, that is my name.
   Aga. What's your affair, I pray you?

260. **on the attentive bent:** to an attentive attitude.

268. **mettle:** spirit.

273. **resty:** inactive; sluggish.

280. **truant:** idle; insincere; **her own lips he loves:** i.e., the lips of his mistress.

282. **other arms:** i.e., martial arms; armor.

284. **make it good:** prove it.

Aen. Sir, pardon: 'tis for Agamemnon's ears.   255

Aga. He hears naught privately that comes from
    Troy.

Aen. Nor I from Troy come not to whisper him.
I bring a trumpet to awake his ear,
To set his sense on the attentive bent,   260
And then to speak.

Aga.   Speak frankly as the wind.
It is not Agamemnon's sleeping hour:
That thou shalt know, Trojan, he is awake,
He tells thee so himself.   265

Aen.   Trumpet, blow loud,
Send thy brass voice through all these lazy tents;
And every Greek of mettle, let him know
What Troy means fairly shall be spoke aloud.

                          Sound trumpet.

We have, great Agamemnon, here in Troy   270
A prince called Hector—Priam is his father—
Who in this dull and long-continued truce
Is resty grown. He bade me take a trumpet
And to this purpose speak. Kings, princes, lords!
If there be one among the fair'st of Greece   275
That holds his honor higher than his ease,
That seeks his praise more than he fears his peril,
That knows his valor and knows not his fear,
That loves his mistress more than in confession
With truant vows to her own lips he loves,   280
And dare avow her beauty and her worth
In other arms than hers—to him this challenge.
Hector, in view of Trojans and of Greeks,
Shall make it good, or do his best to do it,

292. **sunburnt:** dark, therefore unbeautiful by Elizabethan standards.

293. **Even so much:** so much for my message.

295. **soul in such a kind:** feelings that respond to a challenge of this sort.

296. **them:** i.e., all true lovers.

297. **recreant:** coward.

306. **beaver:** part of a helmet covering the lower face.

307. **vantbrace:** armor for the arm; **brawn:** muscle.

310. **His youth in flood:** although he (Hector) is in the full tide of youth.

312. **forfend:** forbid.

He hath a lady, wiser, fairer, truer,   285
Than ever Greek did compass in his arms;
And will tomorrow with his trumpet call
Midway between your tents and walls of Troy,
To rouse a Grecian that is true in love.
If any come, Hector shall honor him;   290
If none, he'll say in Troy when he retires
The Grecian dames are sunburnt and not worth
The splinter of a lance. Even so much.
  Aga. This shall be told our lovers, Lord Aeneas.
If none of them have soul in such a kind,   295
We left them all at home. But we are soldiers;
And may that soldier a mere recreant prove,
That means not, hath not, or is not in love!
If then one is, or hath, or means to be,
That one meets Hector; if none else, I am he.   300
  Nes. Tell him of Nestor, one that was a man
When Hector's grandsire sucked. He is old now;
But if there be not in our Grecian host
One noble man that hath one spark of fire
To answer for his love, tell him from me   305
I'll hide my silver beard in a gold beaver,
And in my vantbrace put this withered brawn,
And meeting him will tell him that my lady
Was fairer than his grandam and as chaste
As may be in the world. His youth in flood,   310
I'll prove this truth with my three drops of blood.
  Aen. Now Heavens forfend such scarcity of youth!
  Uly. Amen.
  Aga. Fair Lord Aeneas, let me touch your hand.
To our pavilion shall I lead you first.   315

322. **young conception:** new idea.

326. **Blunt wedges rive hard knots:** proverbial: knotty problems require extreme measures for their solution; **seeded:** full of seeds soon to be distributed.

328. **rank:** overgrown; uncontrolled.

328-29. **or . . ./ Or:** either . . . or.

335-37. **perspicuous even as substance,/ Whose grossness little characters sum up:** evident as material wealth, the size of which is signified by small numerals.

338. **publication:** proclamation (of the challenge); **make no strain:** have no doubt.

344. **wake him to the answer:** rouse him to answer the challenge.

345. **meet:** suitable; **oppose:** set in opposition (to Hector).

Achilles shall have word of this intent;
So shall each lord of Greece, from tent to tent.
Yourself shall feast with us before you go,
And find the welcome of a noble foe.   *Exeunt.*
                                    Manent Ulysses and Nestor.

Uly. Nestor!   320
Nes. What says Ulysses?
Uly. I have a young conception in my brain:
Be you my Time to bring it to some shape.
Nes. What is't?
Uly. This 'tis: 325
Blunt wedges rive hard knots. The seeded pride
That hath to this maturity blown up
In rank Achilles must or now be cropped,
Or, shedding, breed a nursery of like evil,
To overbulk us all.   330
Nes.   Well, and how?
Uly. This challenge that the gallant Hector sends,
However it is spread in general name,
Relates in purpose only to Achilles.
Nes. True. The purpose is perspicuous even as sub- 335
      stance,
Whose grossness little characters sum up;
And, in the publication, make no strain
But that Achilles, were his brain as barren
As banks of Libya—though, Apollo knows,   340
'Tis dry enough—will, with great speed of judgment,
Ay, with celerity, find Hector's purpose
Pointing on him.
Uly. And wake him to the answer, think you?
Nes. Yes, 'tis most meet. Who may you else oppose, 345

346. **bring those honors off:** gain honor for us all.

348. **in . . . much opinion dwells:** on . . . much reputation rests.

349. **taste our dear'st repute:** test our highest reputation.

350. **fin'st:** most discriminating.

351. **imputation:** reputation; **oddly poised:** unevenly balanced; i.e., exposed to unusual hazard.

352. **success:** outcome.

353. **particular:** personal; **give a scantling:** offer an example.

354. **the general:** the army as a whole.

355. **indexes:** signs.

358. **at large:** in full.

361. **Makes merit her election:** chooses on the basis of merit.

363-65. **who miscarrying,/ What heart receives from hence a conqu'ring part/ To steel a strong opinion to themselves:** i.e., if our champion is defeated, what man of the Greek side could take heart from such a defeat to be confident of his own prowess.

366. **Which entertained:** i.e., such confidence (**strong opinion**) being entertained; **limbs are his instruments:** his (the heart so encouraged) strength is so increased that his arms become weapons as formidable as swords and bows.

That can from Hector bring those honors off,
If not Achilles? Though't be a sportful combat,
Yet in this trial much opinion dwells;
For here the Trojans taste our dear'st repute
With their fin'st palate. And, trust to me, Ulysses,   350
Our imputation shall be oddly poised
In this wild action; for the success,
Although particular, shall give a scantling
Of good or bad unto the general;
And in such indexes, although small pricks   355
To their subsequent volumes, there is seen
The baby figure of the giant mass
Of things to come at large. It is supposed
He that meets Hector issues from our choice;
And choice, being mutual act of all our souls,   360
Makes merit her election and doth boil,
As 'twere from forth us all, a man distilled
Out of our virtues; who miscarrying,
What heart receives from hence a conqu'ring part
To steel a strong opinion to themselves?   365
Which entertained, limbs are his instruments,
In no less working than are swords and bows
Directive by the limbs.
   Uly. Give pardon to my speech.
Therefore 'tis meet Achilles meet not Hector.   370
Let us, like merchants, show our foulest wares,
And think, perchance, they'll sell; if not,
The luster of the better shall exceed
By showing the worse first. Do not consent
That ever Hector and Achilles meet;   375
For both our honor and our shame in this

377. **followers:** consequences.
384. **salt:** bitter.
385. **foiled:** defeated.
386. **main opinion:** general reputation.
387. **In taint:** by the disgrace.
388. **blockish:** stupid.
389. **sort:** lot.
390. **allowance:** acknowledgment.
391. **physic:** purge; **Myrmidon:** the followers of Achilles were called Myrmidons.
392. **fall:** drop.
395. **voices:** praise.
396. **go we under our opinion still:** we will still be given the credit.
402. **straight:** immediately.
404. **tarre:** urge.

Are dogged with two strange followers.

   Nes. I see them not with my old eyes. What are
     they?

   Uly. What glory our Achilles shares from Hector,   380
Were he not proud, we all should share with him.
But he already is too insolent;
And it were better parch in Afric sun
Than in the pride and salt scorn of his eyes,
Should he 'scape Hector fair. If he were foiled,   385
Why then we did our main opinion crush
In taint of our best man. No, make a lott'ry;
And by device let blockish Ajax draw
The sort to fight with Hector. Among ourselves
Give him allowance for the better man;   390
For that will physic the great Myrmidon,
Who broils in loud applause, and make him fall
His crest that prouder than blue Iris bends.
If the dull, brainless Ajax come safe off,
We'll dress him up in voices. If he fail,
Yet go we under our opinion still
That we have better men. But, hit or miss,
Our project's life this shape of sense assumes:
Ajax employed plucks down Achilles' plumes.

   Nes. Now, Ulysses, I begin to relish thy advice;   400
And I will give a taste of it forthwith
To Agamemnon. Go we to him straight.
Two curs shall tame each other. Pride alone
Must tarre the mastiffs on, as 'twere their bone.

                       Exeunt.

TROILUS
AND
CRESSIDA

ACT II

[II.i.] Ajax tries in vain to learn the details of a proclamation from Thersites, who insults him and is beaten in return. When Achilles and Patroclus appear, Thersites is equally abusive of them. Finally Achilles tells Ajax that the proclamation concerns Hector's challenge, which he terms "trash." He hints that he would be the man to answer the challenge if the selection were not to be made by lottery. Ajax decides to look further into the matter.

▬▬▬▬▬▬▬▬▬▬▬▬▬▬

2. **biles:** boils.

6. **botchy core:** inflamed boil, discharging matter.

12-3. **mongrel:** presumably a reference to Ajax' Trojan blood.

14. **whinid'st:** unsalted.

18. **without book:** by heart.

19. **murrain:** plague.

[ACT II]

[Scene I. A part of the Grecian Camp.]

Enter Ajax and Thersites.

Ajax. Thersites!

Ther. Agamemnon—how if he had biles—full, all over, generally?

Ajax. Thersites!

Ther. And those biles did run?—Say so: did not the general run then? Were not that a botchy core? 5

Ajax. Dog!

Ther. Then would come some matter from him. I see none now.

Ajax. Thou bitch-wolf's son, canst thou not hear? 10 Feel, then.   *Strikes him.*

Ther. The plague of Greece upon thee, thou mongrel beef-witted lord!

Ajax. Speak then, thou whinid'st leaven, speak. I will beat thee into handsomeness. 15

Ther. I shall sooner rail thee into wit and holiness; but I think thy horse will sooner con an oration than thou learn a prayer without book. Thou canst strike, canst thou? A red murrain o' thy jade's tricks!

25. **porpentine:** porcupine.

29. **incursions:** military expeditions.

33. **Cerberus:** a many-headed dog that guarded the entrance to Hades; **Proserpina:** the beautiful daughter of Ceres, who was abducted by Pluto, ruler of Hades.

37. **Cobloaf:** ill-shapen figure.

38. **pun:** pound.

40. **whoreson:** good-for-nothing.

45. **asinico:** ass, from the Spanish *asnico*.

46-7. **bought and sold:** regarded with contempt.

48. **use to beat:** make a habit of beating.

Cerberus captured by Hercules. From Vincenzo Cartari, *Imagini de gli dei delli antichi* (1615).

Ajax. Toadstool, learn me the proclamation.   20

Ther. Dost thou think I have no sense, thou strikest
me thus?

Ajax. The proclamation!

Ther. Thou art proclaimed a fool, I think.

Ajax. Do not, porpentine, do not: my fingers itch.   25

Ther. I would thou didst itch from head to foot and.
I had the scratching of thee. I would make thee the
loathsomest scab in Greece. When thou art forth in
the incursions thou strikest as slow as another.

Ajax. I say, the proclamation!   30

Ther. Thou grumblest and railest every hour on
Achilles, and thou art as full of envy at his greatness
as Cerberus is at Proserpina's beauty, ay, that thou
barkst at him.

Ajax. Mistress Thersites!   35

Ther. Thou shouldst strike him.

Ajax. Cobloaf!

Ther. He would pun thee into shivers with his fist,
as a sailor breaks a bisouit.

Ajax. [*Beating him*] You whoreson cur!   40

Ther. Do, do.

Ajax. Thou stool for a witch!

Ther. Ay, do, do! Thou sodden-witted lord, thou
hast no more brain than I have in mine elbows. An
asinico may tutor thee. Thou scurvy-valiant ass! thou   45
art here but to thrash Trojans; and thou art bought
and sold among those of any wit, like a barbarian
slave. If thou use to beat me, I will begin at thy heel
and tell what thou art by inches, thou thing of no
bowels, thou!   50

54. Mars his: the old form of the genitive: Mars's.

70. His evasions have ears thus long: his quibbles are asinine; **bobbed:** beaten.

Ajax. You dog!

Ther. You scurvy lord!

Ajax. [*Beating him*] You cur!

Ther. Mars his idiot! Do, rudeness! Do, camel, do, do!   55

Enter Achilles and Patroclus.

Achil. Why, how now, Ajax! Wherefore do ye thus? How now, Thersites! What's the matter, man?

Ther. You see him there, do you?

Achil. Ay, what's the matter?

Ther. Nay, look upon him.   60

Achil. So I do. What's the matter?

Ther. Nay, but regard him well.

Achil. "Well!" Why, so I do.

Ther. But yet you look not well upon him; for, whosomever you take him to be, he is Ajax.   65

Achil. I know that, fool.

Ther. Ay, but that fool knows not himself.

Ajax. Therefore I beat thee.

Ther. Lo, lo, lo, lo, what modicums of wit he utters! His evasions have ears thus long. I have bobbed his   70
brain more than he has beat my bones. I will buy nine sparrows for a penny, and his *pia mater* is not worth the ninth part of a sparrow. This lord, Achilles, Ajax, who wears his wit in his belly and his guts in his head, I'll tell you what I say of him.   75

Achil. What?

Ther. I say, this Ajax—   [*Ajax offers to strike him.*]

87. **set:** oppose.

96. **suff'rance:** suffering.

98. **under an impress:** drafted, with a pun on "impression" (from the beating).

106. **yoke you:** couple you in the same yoke, like a matching pair of dumb beasts.

Achil. Nay, good Ajax.

Ther. Has not so much wit—

Achil. Nay, I must hold you.   80

Ther. As will stop the eye of Helen's needle, for whom he comes to fight.

Achil. Peace, fool!

Ther. I would have peace and quietness, but the fool will not—he there, that he! Look you there!   85

Ajax. O thou damned cur! I shall—

Achil. Will you set your wit to a fool's?

Ther. No, I warrant you; the fool's will shame it.

Patr. Good words, Thersites.

Achil. What's the quarrel?   90

Ajax. I bade the vile owl go learn me the tenor of the proclamation, and he rails upon me.

Ther. I serve thee not.

Ajax. Well, go to, go to.

Ther. I serve here voluntary.   95

Achil. Your last service was suff'rance, 'twas not voluntary: no man is beaten voluntary. Ajax was here the voluntary, and you as under an impress.

Ther. E'en so: a great deal of your wit, too, lies in your sinews, or else there be liars. Hector shall have a 100 great catch, and he knock out either of your brains! 'A were as good crack a fusty nut with no kernel.

Achil. What, with me too, Thersites?

Ther. There's Ulysses and old Nestor, whose wit was moldy ere your grandsires had nails on their 105 toes, yoke you like draught-oxen and make you plow up the wars.

Achil. What? what?

109. **good sooth:** truly.
114. **brach:** bitch.
117. **clodpolls:** blockheads.
121. **Marry:** indeed.
126. **stomach:** courage.

Ther. Yes, good sooth. To, Achilles! To, Ajax! To!

Ajax. I shall cut out your tongue.   110

Ther. 'Tis no matter. I shall speak as much as thou afterward.

Patr. No more words, Thersites. Peace!

Ther. I will hold my peace when Achilles' brach bids me, shall I?   115

Achil. There's for you, Patroclus.

Ther. I will see you hanged like clodpolls ere I come any more to your tents. I will keep where there is wit stirring and leave the faction of fools.   *Exit.*

Patr. A good riddance.   120

Achil. Marry, this, sir, is proclaimed through all our
       host:
That Hector, by the fifth hour of the sun,
Will with a trumpet 'twixt our tents and Troy
Tomorrow morning call some knight to arms   125
That hath a stomach, and such a one that dare
Maintain I know not what: 'tis trash. Farewell.

Ajax. Farewell. Who shall answer him?

Achil. I know not. 'Tis put to lottery. Otherwise
He knew his man.   130

Ajax. Oh, meaning you? I will go learn more of it.
                                          Exeunt.

[II.ii.] Priam reports to his sons, Hector, Troilus, Paris, and the priest Helenus, the gist of a message from Nestor that the delivery of Helen would end the siege. Hector declares that Helen is not worth the many lives already lost, but Troilus insists that honor requires that Troy not relinquish a woman whose beauty is renowned. Priam's daughter Cassandra enters with predictions of the destruction of Troy, which go unheeded. Paris argues that giving up Helen on terms of compulsion would be doubly disgraceful. Hector, despite his feeling that the abduction of another man's wife is wrong, agrees to keep her, since their honor is at stake. Honor and glory outweigh everything else with the Trojan princes.

<hr/>

6. **cormorant:** ravenous.

7. **struck off:** forgiven, like a debt.

9. **As far as toucheth my particular:** insofar as I myself am concerned.

14. **The wound of peace is surety:** the chief danger to peace is safety.

15. **secure:** too confidently relied upon.

16. **tent:** probe.

19. **tithe soul:** soul claimed as a due; **dismes:** tenths. The meaning is that every single soul out of the thousands that war has claimed is **as dear,** etc.

[Scene II.   Troy.   A room in Priam's Palace.]

Enter Priam, Hector, Troilus, Paris, and Helenus.

Pri. After so many hours, lives, speeches spent,
Thus once again says Nestor from the Greeks:
"Deliver Helen, and all damage else,
As honor, loss of time, travail, expense,
Wounds, friends, and what else dear that is consumed   5
In hot digestion of this cormorant war,
Shall be struck off." Hector, what say you to't?
    Hec. Though no man lesser fears the Greeks than I
As far as toucheth my particular,
Yet, dread Priam,   10
There is no lady of more softer bowels,
More spongy to suck in the sense of fear,
More ready to cry out, "Who knows what follows?"
Than Hector is. The wound of peace is surety,
Surety secure; but modest doubt is called   15
The beacon of the wise, the tent that searches
To the bottom of the worst. Let Helen go.
Since the first sword was drawn about this question,
Every tithe soul 'mongst many thousand dismes
Hath been as dear as Helen; I mean, of ours.   20
If we have lost so many tenths of ours,
To guard a thing not ours, nor worth to us,
Had it our name, the value of one ten,
What merit's in that reason which denies

29. **counters:** tokens used in keeping accounts.

30. **The past-proportion of his infinite:** his infinite worth, which is beyond comparison.

32. **diminutive:** belittling.

34. **though:** if; **reasons:** a pun on "raisins," which was similarly pronounced.

36. **Bear the great sway of his affairs:** manage his great affairs.

40. **fur your gloves with reason:** i.e., employ reasons to keep you comfortable and safe.

49. **disorbed:** thrown out of its sphere.

53. **crammed:** fattened, with consequent loss of vitality; **respect:** circumspection; thoughtfulness.

The yielding of her up?   25
  Tro.   Fie, fie, my brother!
Weigh you the worth and honor of a king
So great as our dread father in a scale
Of common ounces? Will you with counters sum
The past-proportion of his infinite?   30
And buckle in a waist most fathomless
With spans and inches so diminutive
As fears and reasons? Fie, for godly shame!
  Hel. No marvel though you bite so sharp at reasons,
You are so empty of them. Should not our father   35
Bear the great sway of his affairs with reasons,
Because your speech hath none that tells him so?
  Tro. You are for dreams and slumbers, brother
    priest:
You fur your gloves with reason. Here are your reà- 40
    sons:
You know an enemy intends you harm;
You know a sword employed is perilous;
And reason flies the object of all harm.
Who marvels then, when Helenus beholds   45
A Grecian and his sword, if he do set
The very wings of reason to his heels
And fly like chidden Mercury from Jove,
Or like a star disorbed? Nay, if we talk of reason,
Let's shut our gates and sleep. Manhood and honor 50
Should have hare hearts, would they but fat their
    thoughts
With this crammed reason. Reason and respect
Make livers pale and lustihood deject.
  Hec. Brother, she is not worth what she doth cost 55

63-4. **is attributive/ To what infectiously itself affects:** lavishes praises on the object of its instinctive inclination.

65. **image of the affected merit:** visible sign of the presence of admirable quality.

67. **will:** appetite.

69. **traded:** experienced.

70. **avoid:** be rid of.

72-3. **There can be no evasion/ To blench from this and to stand firm by honor:** no excuse can be found that will justify shrinking from this and at the same time preserve honor.

75. **remainder viands:** unconsumed food after a feast.

76. **unrespective sieve:** a receptacle that cannot distinguish between foods of different quality but receives all alike.

79. **breath of full consent:** fully voiced approval.

82. **an old aunt:** Priam's sister Hesione, whom Hercules gave to Telamon when her father, Laomedon, broke his word to reward Hercules' rescue of her. Priam's later request that she be allowed to return to Troy was denied. Hesione was literally the aunt of Priam's sons, but the slang meaning "paramour" may also be intended.

The holding.

   Tro.   What's aught but as 'tis válued?

   Hec. But value dwells not in particular will:
It holds his estimate and dignity
As well wherein 'tis precious of itself   60
As in the prizer. 'Tis mad idolatry
To make the service greater than the god;
And the will dotes that is attributive
To what infectiously itself affects,
Without some image of the affected merit.   65

   Tro. I take today a wife, and my election
Is led on in the conduct of my will;
My will enkindled by mine eyes and ears,
Two traded pilots 'twixt the dangerous shores
Of will and judgment. How may I avoid,   70
Although my will distaste what it elected,
The wife I chose? There can be no evasion
To blench from this and to stand firm by honor.
We turn not back the silks upon the merchant
When we have soiled them, nor the remainder viands 75
We do not throw in unrespective sieve
Because we now are full. It was thought meet
Paris should do some vengeance on the Greeks.
Your breath of full consent bellied his sails;
The seas and winds, old wranglers, took a truce   80
And did him service. He touched the ports desired;
And for an old aunt whom the Greeks held captive
He brought a Grecian queen, whose youth and fresh-
    ness
Wrinkles Apollo's and makes stale the morning.   85
Why keep we her? The Grecians keep our aunt.

95. **issue:** result; **proper:** personal; **rate:** criticize.

96. **that never Fortune did:** i.e., more faithless than even Fortune, noted for her fickleness, ever did.

97. **Beggar the estimation:** depreciate the valued object.

101. **did them that disgrace:** i.e., disgraced the Greeks by abducting Helen.

102. **warrant:** justify.

111. **eld:** elders.

113. **betimes:** early.

Is she worth keeping? Why, she is a pearl
Who price hath launched above a thousand ships
And turned crowned kings to merchants.
If you'll avouch 'twas wisdom Paris went,   90
As you must needs, for you all cried, "Go, go!"
If you'll confess he brought home worthy prize—
As you must needs, for you all clapped your hands,
And cried, "Inestimable!"—why do you now
The issue of your proper wisdoms rate   95
And do a deed that never Fortune did,
Beggar the estimation which you prized
Richer than sea and land? Oh, theft most base,
That we have stol'n what we do fear to keep!
But thieves unworthy of a thing so stol'n   100
That in their country did them that disgrace
We fear to warrant in our native place!

   Cas. [*Within*] Cry, Trojans, cry!
   Pri.   What noise? What shriek is this?
   Tro. 'Tis our mad sister, I do know her voice.   105
   Cas. [*Within*] Cry, Trojans!
   Hec. It is Cassandra.

Enter Cassandra, raving, with her hair about her ears.

   Cas. Cry, Trojans, cry! Lend me ten thousand eyes,
And I will fill them with prophetic tears.
   Hec. Peace, sister, peace!   110
   Cas. Virgins and boys, mid-age and wrinkled eld,
Soft infancy, that nothing canst but cry,
Add to my clamors! Let us pay betimes

114. **moiety:** portion.

117. **firebrand brother:** before Paris was born his mother, Hecuba, dreamed that she had given birth to a firebrand that ignited the whole city.

129. **event:** outcome.

132. **distaste:** render offensive.

134. **make it gracious:** lend it grace.

139. **convince:** convict.

141. **attest:** call to witness.

142. **propension:** desire.

A moiety of that mass of moan to come.
Cry, Trojans, cry! Practice your eyes with tears!   115
Troy must not be, nor goodly Ilion stand;
Our firebrand brother, Paris, burns us all.
Cry, Trojans, cry! A Helen and a woe!
Cry, cry! Troy burns, or else let Helen go.   *Exit.*
    Hec. Now, youthful Troilus, do not these high   120
        strains
Of divination in our sister work
Some touches of remorse? Or is your blood
So madly hot that no discourse of reason,
Nor fear of bad success in a bad cause,   125
Can qualify the same?
    Tro.   Why, brother Hector,
We may not think the justness of each act
Such and no other than event doth form it;
Nor once deject the courage of our minds   130
Because Cassandra's mad. Her brainsick raptures
Cannot distaste the goodness of a quarrel
Which hath our several honors all engaged
To make it gracious. For my private part,
I am no more touched than all Priam's sons;   135
And Jove forbid there should be done amongst us
Such things as might offend the weakest spleen
To fight for and maintain!
    Par. Else might the world convince of levity
As well my undertakings as your counsels.   140
But I attest the gods, your full consent
Gave wings to my propension and cut off
All fears attending on so dire a project.
For what, alas, can these my single arms?

145. **propugnation:** defense.

146. **push and enmity:** hostile attack.

148. **pass:** undergo.

150. **retract:** draw back from.

154. **honey . . . gall:** proverbially, "There is no honey without gall."

155. **So to be valiant is no praise at all:** to be valiant in these circumstances merits no praise.

158. **rape:** abduction.

164. **strain:** impulse.

165. **generous:** noble.

175. **glozed:** commented; provided specious interpretation.

What propugnation is in one man's valor,   145
To stand the push and enmity of those
This quarrel would excite? Yet, I protest,
Were I alone to pass the difficulties,
And had as ample power as I have will,
Paris should ne'er retract what he hath done   150
Nor faint in the pursuit.
   Pri.   Paris, you speak
Like one besotted on your sweet delights.
You have the honey still, but these the gall:
So to be valiant is no praise at all.   155
   Par. Sir, I propose not merely to myself
The pleasures such a beauty brings with it;
But I would have the soil of her fair rape
Wiped off in honorable keeping her.
What treason were it to the ransacked queen,   160
Disgrace to your great worths, and shame to me,
Now to deliver her possession up
On terms of base compulsion! Can it be
That so degenerate a strain as this
Should once set footing in your generous bosoms?   165
There's not the meanest spirit on our party,
Without a heart to dare, or sword to draw,
When Helen is defended, nor none so noble
Whose life were ill bestowed or death unfamed,
Where Helen is the subject. Then, I say,   170
Well may we fight for her, whom, we know well,
The world's large spaces cannot parallel.
   Hec. Paris and Troilus, you have both said well;
And on the cause and question now in hand
Have glozed, but superficially; not much   175

176. **Aristotle:** in his *Nicomachean Ethics.* Many commentators have been disturbed because the relevant phrase, literally translated, referred to "political" philosophy, but Aristotle's discussion in reality concerns what later came to be known as "moral" philosophy.

178-79. **do more conduce/ To the hot passion of distempered blood:** are better calculated to stir the blood.

187. **affection:** perverse inclination.

188. **of:** as a result of.

199. **in way of truth:** as far as abstract justice is concerned.

200. **spritely:** spirited.

200-1. **I propend to you/ In resolution:** I incline to your resolution.

202-3. **hath no mean dependence/ Upon:** has no small connection with.

203. **dignities:** honors.

Unlike young men, whom Aristotle thought
Unfit to hear moral philosophy.
The reasons you allege do more conduce
To the hot passion of distempered blood
Than to make up a free determination   180
'Twixt right and wrong; for pleasure and revenge
Have ears more deaf than adders to the voice
Of any true decision. Nature craves
All dues be rendered to their owners. Now,
What nearer debt in all humanity   185
Than wife is to the husband? If this law
Of nature be corrupted through affection,
And that great minds, of partial indulgence
To their benumbed wills, resist the same,
There is a law in each well-ordered nation   190
To curb those raging appetites that are
Most disobedient and refractory.
If Helen, then, be wife to Sparta's king,
As it is known she is, these moral laws
Of nature and of nations speak aloud   195
To have her back returned. Thus to persist
In doing wrong extenuates not wrong
But makes it much more heavy. Hector's opinion
Is this in way of truth. Yet, ne'ertheless,
My spritely brethren, I propend to you   200
In resolution to keep Helen still;
For 'tis a cause that hath no mean dependence
Upon our joint and several dignities.

    Tro. Why, there you touched the life of our design.
Were it not glory that we more affected   205
Than the performance of our heaving spleens,

210. **magnanimous:** great-souled; lofty in courage.

219. **roisting:** boastful.

220. **dull:** inactive; sluggish.

222. **advertised:** informed.

223. **emulation:** envious rivalry.

▬▬▬▬▬▬▬▬▬▬▬▬▬▬▬▬▬▬▬▬▬▬▬▬

[**II.iii.**] Agamemnon, accompanied by Ulysses, Nestor, Diomedes, Ajax, and Calchas, call at the tent of Achilles. Patroclus reports that Achilles is ill, and Ulysses enters his tent to speak with him. Achilles refuses to fight the next day, with no other excuse than that he does not choose to do so. When Agamemnon proposes that Ajax try to persuade Achilles, Ulysses replies that it would be beneath Ajax' dignity. The rest continue to flatter Ajax, who swells visibly under their words.

▬▬▬▬▬▬▬▬▬▬▬▬▬▬▬▬▬▬

5. **'Sfoot:** God's foot.

44

I would not wish a drop of Trojan blood
Spent more in her defense. But, worthy Hector,
She is a theme of honor and renown;
A spur to valiant and magnanimous deeds,   210
Whose present courage may beat down our foes,
And Fame in time to come canonize us.
For, I presume, brave Hector would not lose
So rich advantage of a promised glory
As smiles upon the forehead of this action   215
For the wide world's revenue.
    Hec.   I am yours,
You valiant offspring of great Priamus.
I have a roisting challenge sent amongst
The dull and factious nobles of the Greeks,   220
Will strike amazement to their drowsy spirits.
I was advertised their great general slept,
Whilst emulation in the army crept.
This, I presume, will wake him.

                                                Exeunt.

[Scene III. The Grecian Camp. Before Achilles' tent.]

Enter Thersites, solus.

    Ther. How now, Thersites! What, lost in the laby-
rinth of thy fury! Shall the elephant Ajax carry it
thus? He beats me, and I rail at him. Oh, worthy satis-
faction! Would it were otherwise: that I could beat
him, while he railed at me. 'Sfoot, I'll learn to conjure   5
and raise devils but I'll see some issue of my spiteful

7. **enginer:** engineer (who lays land mines); contriver.

12. **caduceus:** a staff on which two serpents intertwined.

16. **massy irons:** massive swords.

18. **Neapolitan boneache:** syphilis, sometimes said to have originated in Naples.

20. **placket:** petticoat opening, hence, woman.

25. **slipped:** pun on the word "slip," a **gilt counterfeit** (counterfeit coin covered with silver).

26. **thyself upon thyself:** may you be cursed with yourself.

28. **revenue:** incoming; receipt.

30. **blood:** passions.

32. **lazars:** lepers.

Jove, throwing thunderbolts. From Vincenzo Cartari, *Imagini de gli dei delli antichi* (1615).

execrations. Then there's Achilles, a rare enginer. If
Troy be not taken till these two undermine it, the
walls will stand till they fall of themselves. O thou
great thunderdarter of Olympus, forget that thou art 10
Jove, the king of gods, and, Mercury, lose all the ser-
pentine craft of thy caduceus, if ye take not that little
little less than little wit from them that they have!
which short-armed ignorance itself knows is so abun-
dant scarce it will not in circumvention deliver a fly 15
from a spider without drawing their massy irons and
cutting the web. After this, the vengeance on the
whole camp! or, rather, the Neapolitan boneache! for
that, methinks, is the course depending on those that
war for a placket. I have said my prayers; and devil 20
Envy say Amen. What, ho! my Lord Achilles!

Enter Patroclus.

Patr. Who's there? Thersites! Good Thersites, come
in and rail.
Ther. If I could a remembered a gilt counterfeit,
thou wouldst not have slipped out of my contem- 25
plation; but it is no matter: thyself upon thyself! The
common curse of mankind, folly and ignorance, be
thine in great revenue! Heaven bless thee from a
tutor, and discipline come not near thee! Let thy
blood be thy direction till thy death! Then if she that 30
lays thee out says thou art a fair corse, I'll be sworn
and sworn upon't she never shrouded any but lazars.
Amen. Where's Achilles?
Patr. What, art thou devout? Wast thou in prayer?

40. **my cheese, my digestion:** cheese was considered an aid to digestion.

51. **decline:** recite item by item.

61. **of:** by.

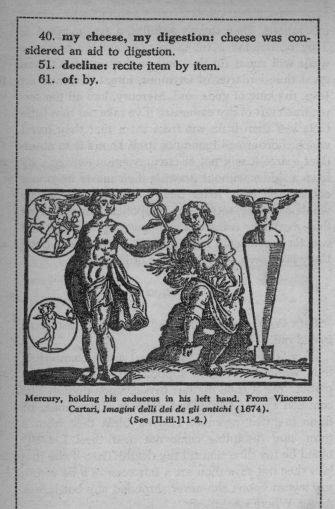

Mercury, holding his caduceus in his left hand. From Vincenzo Cartari, *Imagini delli dei de gli antichi* (1674).
(See [II.iii.]11-2.)

Ther. Ay, the Heavens hear me!   35
Patr. Amen.

Enter Achilles.

Achil. Who's there?
Patr. Thersites, my lord.
Achil. Where? where? Oh, where? Art thou come?
Why, my cheese, my digestion, why hast thou not   40
served thyself in to my table so many meals? Come,
what's Agamemnon?
Ther. Thy commander, Achilles. Then tell me,
Patroclus, what's Achilles?
Patr. Thy lord, Thersites. Then tell me, I pray thee,   45
what's Thersites?
Ther. Thy knower, Patroclus. Then tell me, Patro-
clus, what art thou?
Patr. Thou mayst tell that knowst.
Achil. Oh, tell, tell.   50
Ther. I'll decline the whole question. Agamemnon
commands Achilles; Achilles is my lord; I am Patro-
clus' knower, and Patroclus is a fool.
Patr. You rascal!
Ther. Peace, fool! I have not done.   55
Achil. He is a privileged man. Proceed, Thersites.
Ther. Agamemnon is a fool; Achilles is a fool; Ther-
sites is a fool, and, as aforesaid, Patroclus is a fool.
Achil. Derive this: come!
Ther. Agamemnon is a fool to offer to command   60
Achilles; Achilles is a fool to be commanded of Aga-

69. **patchery:** bungling.

72. **serpigo:** a creeping skin disease, from Latin *serpere*, "to creep."

73. **confound:** destroy.

77. **shent:** scolded.

77-8. **lay by/ Our appertainments, visiting of him:** disregard the dignity proper to ourselves in visiting him.

80. **move the question of our place:** make an issue of our authority.

memnon; Thersites is a fool to serve such a fool; and
this Patroclus is a fool positive.

Patr. Why am I a fool?

Ther. Make that demand to the Creator. It suffices   65
me thou art. Look you, who comes here?

Achil. Patroclus, I'll speak with nobody. Come in
with me, Thersites.   *Exit.*

Ther. Here is such patchery, such juggling, and
such knavery! All the argument is a whore and a   70
cuckold: a good quarrel to draw emulous factions and
bleed to death upon. Now, the dry serpigo on the
subject! and war and lechery confound all!   [*Exit.*]

*Enter Agamemnon, Ulysses, Nestor, Diomedes, Ajax,
and Calchas.*

Aga. Where is Achilles?

Patr. Within his tent, but ill-disposed, my lord.   75

Aga. Let it be known to him that we are here.
He shent our messengers; and we lay by
Our appertainments, visiting of him.
Let him be told so, lest perchance he think
We dare not move the question of our place   80
Or know not what we are.

Patr.   I shall say so to him. [*Exit.*]

Uly. We saw him at the opening of his tent. He is
not sick.

Ajax. Yes, lion-sick, sick of proud heart. You may   85
call it melancholy, if you will favor the man; but, by

93. **matter:** conversational theme.

94. **argument:** (1) subject matter: (2) source of anger.

97. **fraction:** breaking up; dissension.

98. **faction:** partisan alliance; **composure:** composition; compact.

104. **The elephant hath joints:** an erroneous belief persisted, despite the efforts of Aristotle and later scholars to dispel it, that elephants could not bend their knees. See cut.

108. **noble state:** party of noble statesmen.

111. **breath:** breathing; exercise.

The elephant in this cut, presumably because he could not bend his knees, leaned against a tree to sleep, but the tree had been sawed so that his weight pulled it down and he was at the mercy of his enemy. From Geoffrey Whitney, *A Choice of Emblems* (1586).

my head, 'tis pride. But why, why? Let him show us
the cause. A word, my lord.

> [*Takes Agamemnon aside.*]

Nes. What moves Ajax thus to bay at him?

Uly. Achilles hath inveigled his fool from him.   90

Nes. Who, Thersites?

Uly. He.

Nes. Then will Ajax lack matter, if he have lost his
argument.

Uly. No, you see, he is his argument that has his   95
argument: Achilles.

Nes. All the better: their fraction is more our wish
than their faction. But it was a strong composure a
fool could disunite.

Uly. The amity that wisdom knits not, folly may 100
easily untie.

> [*Enter Patroclus.*]

Here comes Patroclus.

Nes. No Achilles with him.

Uly. The elephant hath joints, but none for courtesy. His legs are legs for necessity, not for flexure.   105

Patr. Achilles bids me say he is much sorry
If anything more than your sport and pleasure
Did move your greatness and this noble state
To call upon him. He hopes it is no other
But for your health and your digestion sake,   110
An after-dinner's breath.

Aga.   Hear you, Patroclus:
We are too well acquainted with these answers.

115. **apprehensions:** comprehensions.

116. **attribute:** reputation.

118. **virtuously on his own part beheld:** regarded modestly, as would become a virtuous man.

120. **unwholesome:** dirty.

121. **like:** likely.

124. **under-honest:** lacking in the courtesy proper to an honorable man.

124-25. **in self-assumption greater/ Than in the note of judgment:** more arrogant than wise. Note means distinctive trait.

125. **worthier:** i.e., worthier men.

127. **tend:** wait upon; **savage strangeness:** rude unfriendliness.

128. **Disguise the holy strength of their command:** conceal their authority, which has divine sanction.

129-30. **underwrite in an observing kind/ His humorous predominance:** bow to his perverse assumption of superiority.

135. **engine:** war machine.

136. **lie under this report:** be thus reported.

138. **allowance:** approval.

140. **presently:** at once.

141. **In second voice:** by a spokesman.

But his evasion, winged thus swift with scorn,
Cannot outfly our apprehensions.   115
Much attribute he hath, and much the reason
Why we ascribe it to him. Yet all his virtues,
Not virtuously on his own part beheld,
Do in our eyes begin to lose their gloss,
Yea, like fair fruit in an unwholesome dish,   120
Are like to rot untasted. Go and tell him
We come to speak with him; and you shall not sin
If you do say we think him over-proud
And under-honest; in self-assumption greater
Than in the note of judgment; and worthier than him- 125
    self
Here tend the savage strangeness he puts on,
Disguise the holy strength of their command,
And underwrite in an observing kind
His humorous predominance; yea, watch   130
His course and time, his ebbs and flows, as if
The passage and whole carriage of this action
Rode on his tide. Go tell him this, and add
That if he overhold his price so much,
We'll none of him, but let him, like an engine   135
Not portable, lie under this report:
"Bring action hither, this cannot go to war."
A stirring dwarf we do allowance give
Before a sleeping giant. Tell him so.
    Patr. I shall, and bring his answer presently.   140
                           [Exit.]

    Aga. In second voice we'll not be satisfied.
We come to speak with him. Ulysses, enter you.
                       Exit Ulysses.

148. **subscribe:** endorse.

166. **stream of his dispose:** course that suits his whim.

167. **observance or respect of any:** paying attention to or considering anyone else.

168. **In will peculiar and in self-admission:** in accordance with his personal desire and complacence.

Ajax. What is he more than another?

Aga. No more than what he thinks he is.

Ajax. Is he so much? Do you not think he thinks 145
himself a better man than I am?

Aga. No question.

Ajax. Will you subscribe his thought and say he is?

Aga. No, noble Ajax: you are as strong, as valiant,
as wise, no less noble, much more gentle, and alto- 150
gether more tractable.

Ajax. Why should a man be proud? How doth
pride grow? I know not what pride is.

Aga. Your mind is the clearer, Ajax, and your
virtues the fairer. He that is proud eats up himself. 155
Pride is his own glass, his own trumpet, his own
chronicle; and whatever praises itself but in the deed
devours the deed in the praise.

Ajax. I do hate a proud man, as I do hate the
engend'ring of toads. .   160

Nes. [*Aside*] And yet he loves himself. Is't not
strange?

Enter Ulysses.

Uly. Achilles will not to the field tomorrow.

Aga. What's his excuse?

Uly.   He doth rely on none   165
But carries on the stream of his dispose,
Without observance or respect of any,
In will peculiar and in self-admission.

Aga. Why will he not, upon our fair request,
Untent his person and share the air with us?   170

171-72. **for request's sake only:** only because they were requested.

175. **quarrels at self-breath:** takes exception even to his own words.

178. **Kingdomed Achilles:** i.e., the nature of Achilles, which is likened to a kingdom. Compare *Julius Caesar*, II. i. 67-9; "the state of man/ Like to a little kingdom, suffers then/ The nature of an insurrection." Achilles is at war with himself.

180. **tokens:** the plague was accompanied by spots, known as "tokens," which identified the usually fatal disease.

189. **seam:** lard; fat.

190. **suffers:** allows.

195. **stale his palm:** cheapen his honor. **Palm** is equivalent to "prize," or "military trophy."

196. **assubjugate:** subordinate.

200. **Cancer:** the zodiacal sign, into which the sun enters at the summer solstice, June 21.

201. **Hyperion:** one of the names for the sun-god.

Uly. Things small as nothing, for request's sake
    only,
He makes important. Possessed he is with greatness
And speaks not to himself but with a pride
That quarrels at self-breath. Imagined worth   175
Holds in his blood such swoln and hot discourse
That 'twixt his mental and his active parts
Kingdomed Achilles in commotion rages
And batters down himself. What should I say?
He is so plaguy proud that the death tokens of it   180
Cry, "No recovery."
    Aga.   Let Ajax go to him.
Dear lord, go you and greet him in his tent.
'Tis said he holds you well and will be led
At your request a little from himself.   185
    Uly. O Agamemnon, let it not be so!
We'll consecrate the steps that Ajax makes
When they go from Achilles. Shall the proud lord
That bastes his arrogance with his own seam
And never suffers matter of the world   190
Enter his thoughts, save such as do revolve
And ruminate himself, shall he be worshiped
Of that we hold an idol more than he?
No, this thrice-worthy and right valiant lord
Shall not so stale his palm, nobly acquired,   195
Nor, by my will, assubjugate his merit,
As amply titled as Achilles is,
By going to Achilles.
That were to enlard his fat-already pride
And add more coals to Cancer when he burns   200
With entertaining great Hyperion.

204-5. **rubs the vein of him:** strikes the right note to please Ajax.

211. **feeze:** dispose of; drive away.

217. **The raven chides blackness:** proverbial; compare "The pot calls the kettle black."

218. **let his humors blood:** dispel some of his morbid humor by letting his blood.

229. **force:** farce; stuff.

This lord go to him! Jupiter forbid,
And say in thunder, "Achilles, go to him."

   Nes. [*Aside*] Oh, this is well: he rubs the vein of
     him. 205

   Dio. [*Aside*] And how his silence drinks up this
     applause!

   Ajax. If I go to him, with my armed fist
I'll pash him o'er the face.

   Aga. Oh, no, you shall not go. 210

   Ajax. And 'a be proud with me, I'll feeze his pride.
Let me go to him.

   Uly. Not for the worth that hangs upon our quarrel.

   Ajax. A paltry, insolent fellow!

   Nes. [*Aside*] How he describes himself! 215

   Ajax. Can he not be sociable?

   Uly. [*Aside*] The raven chides blackness.

   Ajax. I'll let his humors blood.

   Aga. [*Aside*] He will be the physician that should
     be the patient. 220

   Ajax. And all men were o' my mind—

   Uly. [*Aside*] Wit would be out of fashion.

   Ajax. 'A should not bear it so; 'a should eat's words
     first.
Shall pride carry it? 225

   Nes. [*Aside*] And 'twould, you'd carry half.

   Uly. [*Aside*] 'A would have ten shares.

   Ajax. I will knead him, I'll make him supple.

   Nes. [*Aside*] He's not yet through warm: force him
with praises. Pour in, pour in; his ambition is dry. 230

   Uly. [*To Agamemnon*] My lord, you feed too much
     on this dislike.

239. **emulous:** envious.

241. **palter:** trifle.

246. **surly borne:** inclined to surly behavior.

247. **strange:** cold; **self-affected:** conceited.

248-49, **of sweet composure:** composed of sweetness; sweet-tempered.

251. **parts of nature:** natural abilities.

256. **Milo:** a strong man of the sixth century B.C., one of whose noted feats was the carrying of an ox; **addition:** title (of strong man).

257. **sinewy:** muscular.

258. **bourn:** boundary; **pale:** fence.

259. **spacious and dilated parts:** spaciously extended (great) endowments.

260. **antiquary times:** i.e., antiquity, into which he has made research.

Nes. Our noble general, do not do so.

Dio. You must prepare to fight without Achilles.

Uly. Why, 'tis this naming of him does him harm.   235
Here is a man—but 'tis before his face:
I will be silent.

Nes.   Wherefore should you so?
He is not emulous, as Achilles is.

Uly. Know the whole world, he is as valiant.   240

Ajax. A whoreson dog, that shall palter thus with
us! Would he were a Trojan!

Nes. What a vice were it in Ajax now—

Uly. If he were proud—

Dio. Or covetous of praise—   245

Uly. Ay, or surly borne—

Dio. Or strange, or self-affected!

Uly. Thank the Heavens, lord, thou art of sweet
   composure;
Praise him that got thee, she that gave thee suck.   250
Famed be thy tutor, and thy parts of nature
Thrice-famed beyond, beyond all erudition.
But he that disciplined thine arms to fight,
Let Mars divide eternity in twain
And give him half. And, for thy vigor,   255
Bull-bearing Milo his addition yield
To sinewy Ajax. I will not praise thy wisdom,
Which, like a bourn, a pale, a shore, confines
Thy spacious and dilated parts. Here's Nestor,
Instructed by the antiquary times,   260
He must, he is, he cannot but be wise;
But pardon, father Nestor, were your days
As green as Ajax', and your brain so tempered,

270. **Please it:** may it please.

271. **state of war:** war council.

274-75. **come knights from east to west/ And cull their flower, Ajax shall cope the best:** Ajax would be a match for the flower of knights come from east or west.

You should not have the eminence of him
But be as Ajax.   265
   Ajax.   Shall I call you father?
   Nes. Ay, my good son.
   Dio.   Be ruled by him, Lord Ajax.
   Uly. There is no tarrying here: the hart Achilles
Keeps thicket. Please it our great general   270
To call together all his state of war.
Fresh kings are come to Troy. Tomorrow
We must with all our main of power stand fast.
And here's a lord, come knights from east to west
And cull their flower, Ajax shall cope the best.   275
   Aga. Go we to council. Let Achilles sleep.
Light boats sail swift, though greater hulks draw
    deep.
                                    Exeunt.

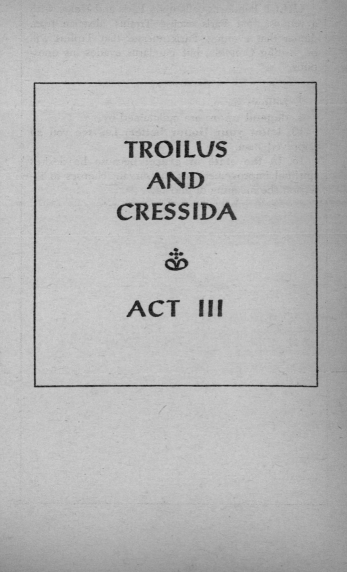

TROILUS
AND
CRESSIDA

ACT III

[III.i.] Pandarus calls upon Paris and Helen with a request that Paris excuse Troilus' absence from dinner that evening. Paris guesses that Troilus will be visiting Cressida, but Pandarus evades his questions.

<hr/>

2. **follow:** serve.

4. **depend upon:** are maintained by.

13. **know your Honor better:** i.e., see you an improved man.

15. **in the state of grace:** because he desires spiritual improvement, as the servant chooses to interpret the meaning of line 14.

[ACT III]

[Scene I. Troy. Priam's Palace.]

Music sounds within. Enter Pandarus and a Servant.

Pan. Friend, you, pray you, a word. Do you not follow the young Lord Paris?

Ser. Ay, sir, when he goes before me.

Pan. You depend upon him, I mean?

Ser. Sir, I do depend upon the Lord. 5

Pan. You depend upon a noble gentleman: I must needs praise him.

Ser. The Lord be praised!

Pan. You know me, do you not?

Ser. Faith, sir, superficially. 10

Pan. Friend, know me better: I am the Lord Pandarus.

Ser. I hope I shall know your Honor better.

Pan. I do desire it.

Ser. You are in the state of grace. 15

Pan. "Grace!" not so, friend: "Honor" and "Lordship" are my titles. What music is this?

Ser. I do but partly know, sir. It is music in parts.

Pan. Know you the musicians?

Ser. Wholly, sir. 20

55

30. **to't:** to the point.
40. **seethes:** boils; stews.
41. **Sodden:** boiled.

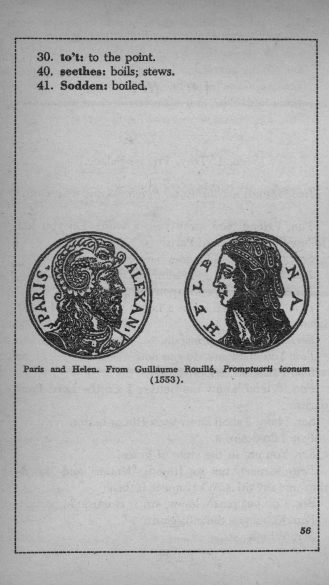

Paris and Helen. From Guillaume Rouillé, *Promptuarii iconum* (1553).

Pan. Who play they to?

Ser. To the hearers, sir.

Pan. At whose pleasure, friend?

Ser. At mine, sir, and theirs that love music.

Pan. Command, I mean, friend.   25

Ser. Who shall I command, sir?

Pan. Friend, we understand not one another. I am too courtly, and thou art too cunning. At whose request do these men play?

Ser. That's to't, indeed, sir. Marry, sir, at the   30 request of Paris, my lord, who is there in person; with him, the mortal Venus, the heartblood of beauty, love's invisible soul.

Pan. Who, my cousin Cressida?

Ser. No, sir, Helen. Could not you find out that by   35 her attributes?

Pan. It should seem, fellow, that thou hast not seen the Lady Cressida. I come to speak with Paris from the Prince Troilus. I will make a complimental assault upon him, for my business seethes.   40

Ser. Sodden business! There's a stewed phrase indeed!

Enter Paris and Helen, [attended].

Pan. Fair be to you, my lord, and to all this fair company! Fair desires, in all fair measure, fairly guide them! especially to you, fair queen! Fair thoughts be   45 your fair pillow!

Helen. Dear lord, you are full of fair words.

49. **broken music:** music played by a "broken," i.e., mixed, group of instruments.

57. **in fits:** in broken phrases.

59. **vouchsafe me a word:** condescend to listen to me briefly.

62. **pleasant:** facetious.

66-7. **commends himself most affectionately to you:** offers you his most affectionate greetings.

68. **bob:** cheat.

Pan. You speak your fair pleasure, sweet queen. Fair prince, here is good broken music.

Par. You have broke it, cousin; and by my life, you 50 shall make it whole again; you shall piece it out with a piece of your performance.

Helen. He is full of harmony.

Pan. Truly, lady, no,

Helen. O sir—   55

Pan. Rude, in sooth: in good sooth, very rude.

Par. Well said, my lord! Well, you say so in fits.

Pan. I have business to my lord, dear queen. My lord, will you vouchsafe me a word?

Helen. Nay, this shall not hedge us out. We'll hear 60 you sing, certainly.

Pan. Well, sweet queen, you are pleasant with me. But, marry, thus, my lord. My dear lord and most esteemed friend, your brother Troilus—

Helen. My Lord Pandarus, honey-sweet lord—   65

Pan. Go to, sweet queen, go to!—commends himself most affectionately to you—

Helen. You shall not bob us out of our melody. If you do, our melancholy upon your head!

Pan. Sweet queen, sweet queen, that's a sweet 70 queen, i' faith.

Helen. And to make a sweet lady sad is a sour offense.

Pan. Nay, that shall not serve your turn; that shall it not, in truth, la. Nay, I care not for such words; no, 75 no. And, my lord, he desires you, that if the King call for him at supper, you will make his excuse.

Helen. My Lord Pandarus—

87. **my disposer Cressida:** i.e., Cressida, who appears to Paris one disposed to pleasure or likely to cause others to be so disposed.

101. **twain:** incompatible.

102-3. **Falling in after falling out may make them three:** a reference to a proverbial saying, "The falling out of lovers is a renewing of love"—which may result in a child.

108. **you may:** you may make fun of me at your pleasure.

Pan. What says my sweet queen, my very, very sweet queen?   80

Par. What exploit's in hand? Where sups he tonight?

Helen. Nay, but, my lord—

Pan. What says my sweet queen? My cousin will fall out with you.   85

Helen. You must not know where he sups.

Par. I'll lay my life, with my disposer Cressida.

Pan. No, no, no such matter; you are wide. Come, your disposer is sick.

Par. Well, I'll make excuse.   90

Pan. Ay, good my lord. Why should you say Cressida? No, your poor disposer's sick.

Par. I spy!

Pan. You spy! What do you spy? Come, give me an instrument. Now, sweet queen.   95

Helen. Why, this is kindly done.

Pan. My niece is horribly in love with a thing you have, sweet queen.

Helen. She shall have it, my lord, if it be not my lord Paris.   100

Pan. He! no, she'll none of him: they two are twain.

Helen. Falling in after falling out may make them three.

Pan. Come, come, I'll hear no more of this. I'll sing you a song now.   105

Helen. Ay, ay, prithee now. By my troth, sweet lord, thou hast a fine forehead.

Pan. Ay, you may, you may.

112. **good now:** if you will be so good.

119. **sore:** wound, with a play on the term for a buck of the fourth year.

133. **a generation of vipers:** Matt. 3:7.

Helen. Let thy song be love: this love will undo us all. O Cupid, Cupid, Cupid! 110

Pan. Love! ay, that it shall, i'faith.

Par. Ay, good now, love, love, nothing but love.

Pan. In good troth, it begins so. *Sings.*

Love, love, nothing but love, still love, still more!
    For, oh, love's bow 115
    Shoots buck and doe:
    The shaft confounds
    Not that it wounds,
But tickles still the sore.
These lovers cry, oh! ho! they die! 120
    Yet that which seems the wound to kill
Doth turn oh! ho! to ha! ha! he!
  So dying love lies still.
Oh! ho! a while, but ha! ha! ha!
Oh! oh! groans out for ha! ha! ha!—hey ho! 125

Helen. In love, i' faith, to the very tip of the nose.

Par. He eats nothing but doves, love, and that breeds hot blood, and hot blood begets hot thoughts, and hot thoughts beget hot deeds, and hot deeds is love. 130

Pan. Is this the generation of love! hot blood, hot thoughts and hot deeds? Why, they are vipers. Is love a generation of vipers? [*To Paris*] Sweet lord, who's afield today?

Par. Hector, Deiphobus, Helenus, Antenor, and all 135 the gallantry of Troy. I would fain have armed today, but my Nell would not have it so. [*To Pandarus*] How chance my brother Troilus went not?

142. **sped:** succeeded.
158. **more palm:** a greater prize.

[III.ii.] Pandarus has at last brought Troilus and Cressida together. Cressida is still coy but confesses her love and both vow eternal fidelity. Pandarus has a chamber available where they may spend the night together.

Helen. He hangs the lip at something. You know
all, Lord Pandarus!   140

Pan. Not I, honey-sweet queen. I long to hear how
they sped today. [*To Paris*] You'll remember your
brother's excuse?

Par. [*To Pandarus*] To a hair.

Pan. Farewell, sweet queen.   145

Helen. Commend me to your niece.

Pan. I will, sweet queen.   [*Exit.*] *Sound a retreat.*

Par. They're come from the field. Let us to Priam's
   hall
To greet the warriors. Sweet Helen, I must woo you   150
To help unarm our Hector. His stubborn buckles,
With these your white enchanting fingers touched,
Shall more obey than to the edge of steel
Or force of Greekish sinews. You shall do more
Than all the island kings: disarm great Hector.   155

Helen. 'Twill make us proud to be his servant, Paris:
Yea, what he shall receive of us in duty
Gives us more palm in beauty than we have,
Yea, overshines ourself.

Par. Sweet, above thought I love thee.   160

                                            Exeunt.

[Scene II. The same. Pandarus' orchard.]

Enter Pandarus and Troilus' Man.

Pan. How now! Where's thy master? At my cousin
   Cressida's?

10. **upon the Stygian banks/ Staying for waftage:** departed souls had to be transported across the river Styx in Hades by Charon.

12. **those fields:** the Elysian Fields.

19. **relish:** taste.

21. **wat'ry:** watering.

22. **thrice-repured:** of a purity many times refined.

23. **Swooning destruction:** obliteration of the senses in a faint.

27. **distinction:** ability to distinguish.

Man. No, sir. He stays for you to conduct him thither.

Pan. Oh, here he comes.   5

Enter Troilus.

How now, how now!

Tro. Sirrah, walk off.   [*Exit Man.*]

Pan. Have you seen my cousin?

Tro. No, Pandarus. I stalk about her door,
Like a strange soul upon the Stygian banks   10
Staying for waftage. Oh, be thou my Charon,
And give me swift transportance to those fields
Where I may wallow in the lily beds
Proposed for the deserver! O gentle Pandar,
From Cupid's shoulder pluck his painted wings   15
And fly with me to Cressid!

Pan. Walk here i' the orchard; I'll bring her straight.
    Exit.

Tro. I am giddy: expectation whirls me round.
The imaginary relish is so sweet
That it enchants my sense. What will it be   20
When that the wat'ry palate tastes indeed
Love's thrice-repured nectar? Death, I fear me,
Swooning destruction, or some joy too fine,
Too subtle-potent, tuned too sharp in sweetness
For the capacity of my ruder powers.   25
I fear it much, and I do fear besides
That I shall lose distinction in my joys,
As doth a battle when they charge on heaps
The enemy flying.

32-3. frayed with a sprite: frightened by a spirit.

37. bestowing: ability to perform.

43. watched: kept sleepless. One method of taming hawks was to tire them by keeping them awake for long periods.

45. fills: shafts (in which draught animals were yoked).

46. curtain: i.e., a face veil.

48. close: come together.

49. rub on, and kiss the mistress: in bowls, the ball was called the "master" or "mistress"; a **rub** was an obstacle in the course.

50. fee-farm: perpetuity; a legal term for a grant of lands in perpetuity.

52. The falcon as the tercel: a **falcon** is the female, a **tercel** the male, peregrine falcon. Pandarus exclaims that he will back his niece to be a match for Troilus.

Enter Pandarus.

Pan. She's making her ready; she'll come straight. 30
You must be witty now. She does so blush, and
fetches her wind so short, as if she were frayed with
a sprite. I'll fetch her. It is the prettiest villain. She
fetches her breath as short as a new-ta'en sparrow.
Exit.

Tro. Even such a passion doth embrace my bosom: 35
My heart beats thicker than a feverous pulse;
And all my powers do their bestowing lose,
Like vassalage at unawares encount'ring
The eye of majesty.

Enter Pandarus and Cressida.

Pan. Come, come, what need you blush? Shame's a 40
baby. Here she is now. Swear the oaths now to her
that you have sworn to me. What, are you gone again?
You must be watched ere you be made tame, must
you? Come your ways, come your ways: and you
draw backward, we'll put you i' the fills. Why do you 45
not speak to her? Come, draw this curtain, and let's
see your picture. Alas the day, how loath you are to
offend daylight! And 'twere dark, you'd close sooner.
So, so: rub on, and kiss the mistress. How now! a kiss
in fee-farm! Build there, carpenter: the air is sweet. 50
Nay, you shall fight your hearts out ere I part you.
The falcon as the tercel, for all the ducks i' the river!
Go to, go to.

57-8. **"In witness whereof the parties inter-changeably"**: phraseology of a legal agreement.

64. **abruption**: abruptness; incoherence; **curious**: suspicious.

79. **will**: desire.

Tro. You have bereft me of all words, lady.

Pan. Words pay no debts, give her deeds. But she'll 55
bereave you o' the deeds too, if she call your activity
in question. What, billing again? Here's "In witness
whereof the parties interchangeably"—Come in, come
in. I'll go get a fire.   *Exit.*

Cres. Will you walk in, my lord?   60

Tro. O Cressida, how often have I wished me thus!

Cres. Wished, my lord? The gods grant—O my lord!

Tro. What should they grant? What makes this
pretty abruption? What too curious dreg espies my
sweet lady in the fountain of our love?   65

Cres. More dregs than water, if my fears have eyes.

Tro. Fears make devils of cherubins: they never see
truly.

Cres. Blind fear, that seeing reason leads, finds
safer footing than blind reason stumbling without 70
fear. To fear the worst oft cures the worse.

Tro. Oh, let my lady apprehend no fear. In all
Cupid's pageant there is presented no monster.

Cres. Nor nothing monstrous neither?

Tro. Nothing but our undertakings, when we vow 75
to weep seas, live in fire, eat rocks, tame tigers, thinking it harder for our mistress to devise imposition
enough than for us to undergo any difficulty imposed.
This is the monstruosity in love, lady, that the will is
infinite and the execution confined; that the desire is 80
boundless and the act a slave to limit.

Cres. They say all lovers swear more performance
than they are able and yet reserve an ability that
they never perform, vowing more than the perfection

88-9. **Praise us as we are tasted, allow us as we prove:** compare the proverb "Praise at parting," a caution not to judge rashly.

90. **in reversion:** due to revert to one in the future; in legal terminology, the right of inheritance or succession to an office.

92-3. **addition:** title.

93. **Few words to fair faith:** compare the proverb "Where many words are, the truth goes by."

94-5. **what envy can say worst shall be a mock for his truth:** malice will be able to find nothing to criticize and will have to be content to mock his fidelity.

100. **folly:** wantonness; loss of chastity.

102. **get:** beget.

of ten and discharging less than the tenth part of one.   85
They that have the voice of lions and the act of hares,
are they not monsters?

Tro. Are there such? Such are not we. Praise us as
we are tasted, allow us as we prove. Our head shall
go bare till merit crown it. No perfection in reversion   90
shall have a praise in present. We will not name
desert before his birth, and, being born, his addition shall be humble. Few words to fair faith. Troilus
shall be such to Cressid as what envy can say worst
shall be a mock for his truth, and what truth can   95
speak truest not truer than Troilus.

Cres. Will you walk in, my lord?

Enter Pandarus.

Pan. What, blushing still? Have you not done talking yet?

Cres. Well, uncle, what folly I commit, I dedicate   100
to you.

Pan. I thank you for that. If my lord get a boy of
you, you'll give him me. Be true to my lord. If he
flinch, chide me for it.

Tro. You know now your hostages: your uncle's   105
word and my firm faith.

Pan. Nay, I'll give my word for her too. Our
kindred, though they be long ere they be wooed, they
are constant being won. They are burs, I can tell you:
they'll stick where they are thrown.   110

Cres. Boldness comes to me now and brings me
    heart.

132. My very soul of counsel: the inmost secrets of my soul.

Prince Troilus, I have loved you night and day
For many weary months.

 Tro. Why was my Cressid then so hard to win? 115

 Cres. Hard to seem won. But I was won, my lord,
With the first glance that ever—pardon me:
If I confess much, you will play the tyrant.
I love you now, but till now not so much
But I might master it. In faith, I lie: 120
My thoughts were, like unbridled children, grown
Too headstrong for their mother. See, we fools!
Why have I blabbed? Who shall be true to us
When we are so unsecret to ourselves?
But, though I loved you well, I wooed you not; 125
And yet, good faith, I wished myself a man,
Or that we women had men's privilege
Of speaking first. Sweet, bid me hold my tongue;
For in this rapture I shall surely speak
The thing I shall repent. See, see, your silence, 130
Cunning in dumbness, from my weakness draws
My very soul of counsel! Stop my mouth.

 Tro. And shall, albeit sweet music issues thence.

 Pan. Pretty, i' faith.

 Cres. My lord, I do beseech you, pardon me: 135
'Twas not my purpose thus to beg a kiss.
I am ashamed. O Heavens! what have I done?
For this time will I take my leave, my lord.

 Tro. Your leave, sweet Cressid?

 Pan. Leave! and you take leave till tomorrow 140
morning—

 Cres. Pray you, content you.

 Tro.   What offends you, lady?

155. **roundly:** frankly.

157-58. **to be wise and love/ Exceeds man's might: that dwells with gods above:** a proverbial idea.

162. **in plight and youth:** as fresh as when it was plighted.

163. **outward:** external appearance.

167. **affronted:** confronted; matched; **match and weight:** matching weight.

168. **winnowed:** sifted; refined.

    Cres. Sir, mine own company.

    Tro. You cannot shun yourself.   145

    Cres. Let me go and try.

I have a kind of self resides with you,

But an unkind self that itself will leave

To be another's fool. I would be gone.

Where is my wit? I know not what I speak.   150

    Tro. Well know they what they speak that speak so
      wisely.

    Cres. Perchance, my lord, I show more craft than
      love

And fell so roundly to a large confession   155

To angle for your thoughts. But you are wise;

Or else you love not, for to be wise and love

Exceeds man's might: that dwells with gods above.

    Tro. Oh that I thought it could be in a woman—

As, if it can, I will presume in you—   160

To feed for aye her lamp and flames of love;

To keep her constancy in plight and youth,

Outliving beauty's outward, with a mind

That doth renew swifter than blood decays!

Or that persuasion could but thus convince me   165

That my integrity and truth to you

Might be affronted with the match and weight

Of such a winnowed purity in love:

How were I then uplifted! But, alas!

I am as true as truth's simplicity   170

And simpler than the infancy of truth.

    Cres. In that I'll war with you.

    Tro.   O virtuous fight,

When right with right wars who shall be most right!

176. **Approve:** demonstrate; prove.

179. **as plantage to the moon:** referring to the moon's influence on crops.

180. **turtle:** turtledove.

183. **As truth's authentic author to be cited:** as though citing truth's most authentic example.

185. **numbers:** rhymes.

191. **characterless:** unmarked.

197. **Pard:** panther.

198. **stick:** transfix.

True swains in love shall in the world to come   175
Approve their truth by Troilus. When their rhymes,
Full of protest, of oath and big compare,
Want similes, truth tired with iteration—
"As true as steel, as plantage to the moon,
As sun to day, as turtle to her mate,   180
As iron to adamant, as earth to the center"—
Yet, after all comparisons of truth,
As truth's authentic author to be cited,
"As true as Troilus" shall crown up the verse
And sanctify the numbers.   185
   Cres.   Prophet may you be!
If I be false, or swerve a hair from truth,
When Time is old and hath forgot itself,
When waterdrops have worn the stones of Troy,
And blind oblivion swallowed cities up,   190
And mighty states characterless are grated
To dusty nothing, yet let memory,
From false to false, among false maids in love,
Upbraid my falsehood! when th' have said "As false
As air, as water, wind, or sandy earth,   195
As fox to lamb, or wolf to heifer's calf,
Pard to the hind, or stepdame to her son"—
"Yea," let them say, to stick the heart of falsehood,
"As false as Cressid."
   Pan. Go to, a bargain made. Seal it, seal it! I'll be   200
the witness. Here I hold your hand; here my cousin's.
If ever you prove false one to another, since I have
taken such pains to bring you together, let all pitiful
goers-between be called to the world's end after my
name: call them all Pandars. Let all constant men be   205

211. **because:** in order that. There is a pun on the penalty for refusing to plead in a criminal action: pressing to death by weights.

━━━━━━━━━━━━━━━━━━━━━━━━━━━━━━━━

[III.iii.] Calchas, a seer who abandoned Troy to serve the Greeks, asks that his daughter Cressida be exchanged for some Trojan captive. The Trojans have refused to give her up in exchange for other prisoners, but he feels that the recently captured Antenor is so highly valued that Cressida may be exchanged for him. Seeing Achilles, standing in his tent door with Patroclus, the Greek leaders follow Ulysses' advice to ignore him. Achilles is nettled at their coldness; Ulysses gives him a lecture emphasizing that past deeds are soon forgotten and virtue must be exercised. He points out that slow-witted Ajax is receiving a hero's due because he is playing the part of a hero. Achilles' love for Priam's daughter Polyxena is known to the Greeks, Ulysses reveals, and it would be shameful to let it be said that Achilles was won by Hector's sister, while Ajax defeated the Trojan hero.

Troiluses, all false women Cressids, and all brokers-
between Pandars! Say "Amen."

Tro. Amen.

Cres. Amen.

Pan. Amen. Whereupon I will show you a chamber, 210
whose bed, because it shall not speak of your pretty
encounters, press it to death, Away!

      Exeunt [Troilus and Cressida].

And Cupid grant all tongue-tied maidens here

Bed, chamber, Pandar to provide this gear! *Exit.*

[Scene III. The Grecian Camp. Before Achilles' tent.]

*Flourish. Enter Ulysses, Diomedes, Nestor,
Agamemnon, Ajax, Menelaus, and Calchas.*

Cal. Now, princes, for the service I have done,
The advantage of the time prompts me aloud
To call for recompense. Appear it to your mind
That, through the sight I bear in things to come,
I have abandoned Troy, left my possession,   5
Incurred a traitor's name, exposed myself,
From certain and possessed conveniences,
To doubtful fortunes, sequest'ring from me all
That time, acquaintance, custom, and condition
Made tame and most familiar to my nature,   10
And here, to do you service, am become
As new into the world, strange, unacquainted.
I do beseech you, as in way of taste,
To give me now a little benefit

16. **live:** are already available.

22. **in right great exchange:** in exchange for some particularly distinguished Trojan prisoner.

23. **still:** always.

24. **wrest:** tuning-key; i.e., one who promotes harmony.

31. **In most accepted pain:** with hardship endured most patiently.

35. **Furnish you fairly:** see that you are adequately equipped.

41. **strangely:** coldly.

Ulysses and Diomedes. From Geoffrey Whitney, *A Choice of Emblems* (1586).

Out of those many registered in promise,   15
Which, you say, live to come in my behalf.
  Aga. What wouldst thou of us, Trojan? Make
    demand.
  Cal. You have a Trojan prisoner, called Antenor,
Yesterday took. Troy holds him very dear.   20
Oft have you—often have you thanks therefor—
Desired my Cressid in right great exchange,
Whom Troy hath still denied; but this Antenor,
I know, is such a wrest in their affairs
That their negotiations all must slack,   25
Wanting his manage; and they will almost
Give us a prince of blood, a son of Priam,
In change of him. Let him be sent, great princes,
And he shall buy my daughter; and her presence
Shall quite strike off all service I have done,   30
In most accepted pain.
  Aga.   Let Diomedes bear him,
And bring us Cressid hither. Calchas shall have
What he requests of us. Good Diomed,
Furnish you fairly for this interchange.   35
Withal, bring word if Hector will tomorrow
Be answered in his challenge. Ajax is ready.
  Dio. This shall I undertake; and 'tis a burden
Which I am proud to bear.
                    [*Exeunt Diomedes and Calchas.*]

  Achilles and Patroclus stand in their tent.

  Uly. Achilles stands i' the entrance of his tent.   40
Please it our general pass strangely by him,

45. unplausive: unflattering: disapproving.

48. To use between your strangeness and his pride: to apply to the wound your coldness will cause.

50-51. Pride hath no other glass/ To show itself but pride: i.e., the proud man can only be made to see himself in the proud behavior of others.

51. supple knees: obsequious behavior.

Hector, Patroclus, and Achilles. From Isaac de la Rivière, *Speculum heroici* (1613).

As if he were forgot; and, princes all,
Lay negligent and loose regard upon him.
I will come last. 'Tis like he'll question me
Why such unplausive eyes are bent, why turned on   45
    him.
If so, I have derision medicinable
To use between your strangeness and his pride,
Which his own will shall have desire to drink.
It may do good. Pride hath no other glass   50
To show itself but pride, for supple knees
Feed arrogance and are the proud man's fees.

    Aga. We'll execute your purpose and put on
A form of strangeness as we pass along:
So do each lord, and either greet him not   55
Or else disdainfully, which shall shake him more
Than if not looked on. I will lead the way.

    Achil. What, comes the general to speak with me?
You know my mind: I'll fight no more 'gainst Troy.

    Aga. What says Achilles? Would he aught with us? 60
    Nes. Would you, my lord, aught with the general?
    Achil. No.
    Nes. Nothing, my lord.
    Aga. The better.

                    [*Exeunt Agamemnon and Nestor.*]
    Achil. Good day, good day.   65
    Men. How do you? How do you?   [*Exit.*]
    Achil. What, does the cuckold scorn me?
    Ajax. How now, Patroclus!
    Achil. Good morrow, Ajax.
    Ajax. Ha?   70
    Achil. Good morrow.

75. **used:** accustomed.

82. **declined:** fallen in favor.

85. **mealy:** powdery, referring to the floury covering of the wings.

88. **without him:** external.

95. **At ample point:** fully.

Thetis, mother of Achilles, mourning at his tomb. From Geoffrey Whitney, *A Choice of Emblems* (1586).

Ajax. Ay, and good next day too.   *Exit.*

Achil. What mean these fellows? Know they not
    Achilles?

Patr. They pass by strangely. They were used to   75
    bend,
To send their smiles before them to Achilles,
To come as humbly as they used to creep
To holy altars.

Achil.   What, am I poor of late?   80
'Tis certain, greatness, once fall'n out with fortune,
Must fall out with men too. What the declined is
He shall as soon read in the eyes of others
As feel in his own fall. For men, like butterflies,
Show not their mealy wings but to the summer;   85
And not a man, for being simply man,
Hath any honor, but honor for those honors
That are without him, as place, riches, and favor,
Prizes of accident as oft as merit:
Which when they fall, as being slippery standers,   90
The love that leaned on them as slippery too,
Doth one pluck down another and together
Die in the fall. But 'tis not so with me.
Fortune and I are friends. I do enjoy
At ample point all that I did possess,   95
Save these men's looks, who do, methinks, find out
Something not worth in me such rich beholding
As they have often given. Here is Ulysses.
I'll interrupt his reading.
How now, Ulysses!   100

Uly.   Now, great Thetis' son!

Achil. What are you reading?

104. **how dearly ever parted**: however amply endowed with parts (qualities; accomplishments).

105. **How much in having**: however wealthy.

107. **owes**: possesses; **by reflection**: this, which repeats the thought of lines 50-1, expresses a proverbial idea, made further explicit in lines 112-20.

113. **commends**: offers.

116-17. **eye to eye opposed/ Salutes each other with each other's form**: i.e., each sees his own reflection in the other's eye.

118. **speculation**: sight.

123. **circumstance**: detailed exposition; elaboration.

125. **in and of him there be much consisting**: he is composed of and responsible for many things.

126. **communicate his parts to others**: share his abilities with others; use his talents for the common good.

129. **extended**: enlarged; **who . . . reverb'rate**: which (applause) echoes.

   Uly.   A strange fellow here
Writes me: "That man, how dearly ever parted,
How much in having, or without or in,   105
Cannot make boast to have that which he hath,
Nor feels not what he owes, but by reflection;
As when his virtues shining upon others
Heat them and they retort that heat again
To the first giver."   110
   Achil.   This is not strange, Ulysses.
The beauty that is borne here in the face
The bearer knows not, but commends itself
To others' eyes. Nor doth the eye itself,
That most pure spirit of sense, behold itself,   115
Not going from itself; but eye to eye opposed
Salutes each other with each other's form.
For speculation turns not to itself
Till it hath traveled and is mirrored there
Where it may see itself. This is not strange at all.   120
   Uly. I do not strain at the position—
It is familiar—but at the author's drift;
Who in his circumstance expressly proves
That no man is the lord of anything,
Though in and of him there be much consisting,   125
Till he communicate his parts to others;
Nor doth he of himself know them for aught,
Till he behold them formed in the applause
Where th' are extended; who, like an arch, reverb'rate
The voice again; or, like a gate of steel   130
Fronting the sun, receives and renders back
His figure and his heat. I was much rapt in this
And apprehended here immediately

134. **unknown Ajax:** i.e., Ajax, who would have been unknown to the author he cites.

137. **abject in regard and dear in use:** poorly regarded but valuable in action.

142. **leave:** cease.

145-46. **eats into another's pride,/ While pride is fasting in his wantonness:** tastes the hero's fame, while the hero nurses his pride and declines to act.

148. **lubber:** lout.

162-63. **mail/ In monumental mock'ry:** armor, in imitation of the armor on a funeral monument.

163. **instant:** nearest.

Time with a wallet at his back. From an antipapal ballad.

The unknown Ajax. Heavens what a man is there!
A very horse that has he knows not what!   135
Nature, what things there are
Most abject in regard and dear in use!
What things again most dear in the esteem
And poor in worth! Now shall we see tomorrow—
An act that very chance doth throw upon him—   140
Ajax renowned. O Heavens, what some men do,
While some men leave to do!
How some men creep in skittish Fortune's hall,
Whiles others play the idiots in her eyes!
How one man eats into another's pride,   145
While pride is fasting in his wantonness!
To see these Grecian lords! Why, even already
They clap the lubber Ajax on the shoulder,
As if his foot were on brave Hector's breast
And great Troy shrieking.   150
    Achil. I do believe it; for they passed by me
As misers do by beggars, neither gave to me
Good word nor look. What, are my deeds forgot?
    Uly. Time hath, my lord, a wallet at his back
Wherein he puts alms for oblivion,   155
A great-sized monster of ingratitudes.
Those scraps are good deeds past, which are de-
    voured
As fast as they are made, forgot as soon
As done. Perseverance, dear my lord,   160
Keeps honor bright. To have done is to hang
Quite out of fashion, like a rusty mail
In monumental mock'ry. Take the instant way;
For honor travels in a strait so narrow

165. **one but goes:** only one goes.

168. **forthright:** straight path.

172. **the abject rear:** the baser ones placed in the rear of the battle line.

186. **One touch of nature makes the whole world kin:** one fault held in common proves the kinship of all mankind.

187. **gawds:** trinkets.

189. **gilt:** gilded.

190. **o'erdusted:** covered with the dust of age.

192. **great and complete:** greatly accomplished.

195. **The cry went once on thee:** you formerly received popular acclaim.

74

Where one but goes abreast. Keep then the path;   165
For emulation hath a thousand sons
That one by one pursue. If you give way,
Or hedge aside from the direct forthright,
Like to an entered tide they all rush by
And leave you hindmost;   170
Or, like a gallant horse fall'n in first rank,
Lie there for pavement to the abject rear,
O'errun and trampled on. Then what they do in
    present,
Though less than yours in past, must o'ertop yours;   175
For time is like a fashionable host
That slightly shakes his parting guest by the hand,
And with his arms outstretched, as he would fly,
Grasps in the comer. The welcome ever smiles,
And farewell goes out sighing. Oh, let not virtue seek   180
Remuneration for the thing it was;
For beauty, wit,
High birth, vigor of bone, desert in service,
Love, friendship, charity, are subjects all
To envious and calumniating Time.   185
One touch of nature makes the whole world kin;
That all with one consent praise newborn gawds,
Though they are made and molded of things past,
And give to dust that is a little gilt
More laud than gilt o'erdusted.   190
The present eye praises the present object.
Then marvel not, thou great and complete man,
That all the Greeks begin to worship Ajax,
Since things in motion sooner catch the eye
Than what stirs not. The cry went once on thee,   195

201. **faction:** taking sides.

211. **Pluto's gold:** Pluto, "giver of wealth," the god of the underworld, controlled the riches to be found in the earth.

212. **uncomprehensive:** unfathomable.

215-16. **with whom relation/ Durst never meddle:** of which men dare not speak.

218. **expressure:** expression.

219. **commerce:** communication; intercourse.

220. **As perfectly is ours as yours:** is as perfectly known to us as it is to you.

222. **Polyxena:** the daughter of Priam referred to in line 207.

223. **Pyrrhus:** Achilles' son.

Mars. From Vincenzo Cartari, *Imagini de gli dei delli antichi* (1615).

And still it might, and yet it may again,
If thou wouldst not entomb thyself alive
And case thy reputation in thy tent,
Whose glorious deeds, but in these fields of late,
Made emulous missions 'mongst the gods themselves   200
And drave great Mars to faction.
  Achil.   Of this my privacy
I have strong reasons.
  Uly.   But 'gainst your privacy
The reasons are more potent and heroical.   205
'Tis known, Achilles, that you are in love
With one of Priam's daughters.
  Achil.   Ha! known?
  Uly. Is that a wonder?
The providence that's in a watchful state   210
Knows almost every grain of Pluto's gold,
Finds bottom in the uncomprehensive deeps,
Keeps place with thought, and almost, like the gods,
Does thoughts unveil in their dumb cradles.
There is a mystery, with whom relation   215
Durst never meddle, in the soul of state;
Which hath an operation more divine
Than breath or pen can give expressure to.
All the commerce that you have had with Troy
As perfectly is ours as yours, my lord;   220
And better would it fit Achilles much
To throw down Hector than Polyxena.
But it must grieve young Pyrrhus now at home,
When Fame shall in our islands sound her trump,
And all the Greekish girls shall tripping sing,   225
"Great Hector's sister did Achilles win,

229. **The fool slides o'er the ice that you should break**: the meaning probably is that Achilles should act to put an end to Ajax' showing off.

230. **moved**: urged.

234. **stomach**: appetite; courage; **to**: for.

243. **shrewdly gored**: sorely wounded.

247. **Seals a commission to a blank of danger**: gives danger a warrant that places one at its mercy. The **blank** is a warrant such as officials were given by the Crown to impower them to act on its behalf.

255. **weeds**: garments.

Polyxena. From Guillaume Rouillé, *Promptuarii iconum* (1553). (See [III.iii.]222.)

But our great Ajax bravely beat down him."
Farewell, my lord. I as your lover speak:
The fool slides o'er the ice that you should break.

Exit.

Patr. To this effect, Achilles, have I moved you.   230
A woman impudent and mannish grown
Is not more loathed than an effeminate man
In time of action. I stand condemned for this.
They think my little stomach to the war
And your great love to me restrains you thus.   235
Sweet, rouse yourself, and the weak wanton Cupid
Shall from your neck unloose his amorous fold,
And, like a dewdrop from the lion's mane,
Be shook to air.

Achil.   Shall Ajax fight with Hector?   240
Patr. Ay, and perhaps receive much honor by him.
Achil. I see my reputation is at stake;
My fame is shrewdly gored.
Patr.   Oh, then, beware:
Those wounds heal ill that men do give themselves.   245
Omission to do what is necessary
Seals a commission to a blank of danger;
And danger, like an ague, subtly taints
Even then when they sit idly in the sun.

Achil. Go call Thersites hither, sweet Patroclus.   250
I'll send the fool to Ajax, and desire him
T' invite the Trojan lords after the combat
To see us here unarmed. I have a woman's longing,
An appetite that I am sick withal,
To see great Hector in his weeds of peace;   255

257. **to my full of view:** as fully as my eyes can wish.

270. **politic regard:** look of shrewdness.

272. **coldly:** sluggishly.

279. **land fish:** i.e., he is out of his element and scarcely knows where he is; **of:** on.

280. **opinion:** judgment; **wear it on both sides:** show it to good and bad advantage at different times.

To talk with him, and to behold his visage,
Even to my full of view.—A labor saved!

Enter Thersites.

Ther. A wonder!

Achil. What?

Ther. Ajax goes up and down the field, asking for 260
himself.

Achil. How so?

Ther. He must fight singly tomorrow with Hector,
and is so prophetically proud of an heroical cudgeling
that he raves in saying nothing. 265

Achil. How can that be?

Ther. Why, 'a stalks up and down like a peacock—
a stride and a stand; ruminates like an hostess that
hath no arithmetic but her brain to set down her
reckoning; bites his lip with a politic regard, as who 270
should say, "There were wit in this head, and 'twould
out." And so there is, but it lies as coldly in him as fire
in a flint, which will not show without knocking.
The man's undone forever, for if Hector break not his
neck i' the combat, he'll break't himself in vainglory. 275
He knows not me. I said, "Good morrow, Ajax"; and
he replies, "Thanks, Agamemnon." What think you of
this man that takes me for the general? He's grown a
very land fish, languageless, a monster. A plague of
opinion! A man may wear it on both sides, like a 280
leather jerkin.

Achil. Thou must be my ambassador to him,
Thersites.

284-85. **professes:** makes a vocation of.

286. **put on:** imitate.

288. **pageant:** spectacle.

311-12. **he shall pay for me ere he has me:** he shall not conquer me easily.

Ther. Who, I? Why, he'll answer nobody; he professes not answering. Speaking is for beggars: he 285
wears his tongue in's arms. I will put on his presence.
Let Patroclus make demands to me, you shall see the
pageant of Ajax.

Achil. To him, Patroclus. Tell him I humbly desire
the valiant Ajax to invite the most valorous Hector to 290
come unarmed to my tent, and to procure safe-
conduct for his person of the magnanimous and most
illustrious six-or-seven-times-honored captain general
of the Grecian army, Agamemnon, et cetera. Do this.

Patr. Jove bless great Ajax!   295

Ther. Hum!

Patr. I come from the worthy Achilles—

Ther. Ha!

Patr. Who most humbly desires you to invite
Hector to his tent—   300

Ther. Hum!

Patr. And to procure safe-conduct from Agamemnon.

Ther. Agamemnon?

Patr. Ay, my lord.   305

Ther. Ha!

Patr. What say you to't?

Ther. God be wi' you, with all my heart.

Patr. Your answer, sir.

Ther. If tomorrow be a fair day, by eleven of the 310
clock it will go one way or other. Howsoever, he shall
pay for me ere he has me.

Patr. Your answer, sir.

Ther. Fare ye well, with all my heart.

319. **catlings:** catgut.
323. **capable:** intelligent.

Apollo with his "fiddle" (actually a lyre). From Giulio Cesare Capaccio, *Gli apologi* (1619).

Achil. Why, but he is not in this tune, is he?   315

Ther. No, but he's out o' tune thus. What music will
be in him when Hector has knocked out his brains,
I know not; but, I am sure, none, unless the fiddler
Apollo get his sinews to make catlings on.

Achil. Come, thou shalt bear a letter to him 320
straight.

Ther. Let me bear another to his horse, for that's
the more capable creature.

Achil. My mind is troubled like a fountain stirred,
And I myself see not the bottom of it.   325

     [Exeunt Achilles and Patroclus.]

Ther. Would the fountain of your mind were clear
again, that I might water an ass at it! I had rather be
a tick in a sheep than such a valiant ignorance.

         [Exit.]

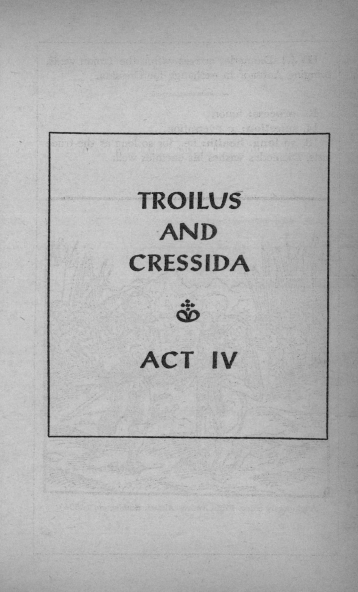

TROILUS
AND
CRESSIDA

❧

ACT IV

[IV.i.] Diomedes arrives within the Trojan walls, bringing Antenor in exchange for Cressida.

▬▬▬▬▬▬▬▬▬▬

10. **procéss:** tenor.

14. **question:** conversation.

18. **so long, health:** i.e., for so long as the truce lasts, Diomedes wishes his enemies well.

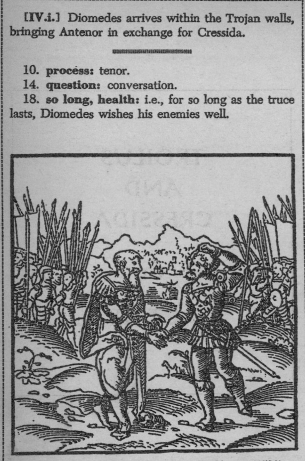

A temporary truce. From Andrea Alciati, *Emblemata* (1534).

[ACT IV]

[Scene I. Troy. A street.]

Enter at one door Aeneas [and Servant] with a
torch; at another, Paris, Deiphobus, Antenor, Dio-
medes the Grecian, [and others,] with torches.

Par. See, ho! who is that there?

Dei. It is the Lord Aeneas.

Aen. Is the Prince there in person?
Had I so good occasion to lie long
As you, Prince Paris, nothing but heavenly business   5
Should rob my bedmate of my company.

Dio. That's my mind too. Good morrow, Lord
   Aeneas.

Par. A valiant Greek, Aeneas—take his hand—
Witness the process of your speech, wherein   10
You told how Diomed a whole week by days
Did haunt you in the field.

Aen. Health to you, valiant sir,
During all question of the gentle truce;
But when I meet you armed, as black defiance   15
As heart can think or courage execute.

Dio. The one and other Diomed embraces.
Our bloods are now in calm, and, so long, health!

19. **when contention and occasion meet:** when the occasion is ripe for combat.

24. **Anchises:** father of Aeneas.

25. **Venus:** mother of Aeneas.

26. **sort:** manner.

29. **If to my sword his fate be not the glory:** if my sword is not to win glory by killing him.

31. **in mine emulous honor:** for the sake of my honor, which depends on my rivalry of him.

34. **worse:** under worse conditions.

40. **His purpose:** i.e., Diomedes.

42. **render:** deliver to.

45. **constantly:** firmly.

49. **quality wherefore:** reason why.

Aeneas bearing Anchises from the burning Troy. From Andrea Alciati, *Emblemata* (1534).

But when contention and occasion meet,
By Jove, I'll play the hunter for thy life   20
With all my force, pursuit, and policy.

Aen. And thou shalt hunt a lion that will fly
With his face backward. In humane gentleness,
Welcome to Troy! Now, by Anchises' life,
Welcome, indeed! By Venus' hand I swear,   25
No man alive can love in such a sort
The thing he means to kill more excellently.

Dio. We sympathize. Jove, let Aeneas live,
If to my sword his fate be not the glory,
A thousand complete courses of the sun!   30
But, in mine emulous honor, let him die,
With every joint a wound, and that tomorrow.

Aen. We know each other well.

Dio. We do, and long to know each other worse.

Par. This is the most despiteful gentle greeting,   35
The noblest hateful love, that e'er I heard of.
What business, lord, so early?

Aen. I was sent for to the King; but why, I know
not.

Par. His purpose meets you. 'Twas to bring this   40
    Greek
To Calchas' house and there to render him,
For the enfreed Antenor, the fair Cressid.
Let's have your company, or, if you please,
Haste there before us. I constantly believe—   45
Or rather call my thought a certain knowledge—
My brother Troilus lodges there tonight.
Rouse him and give him note of our approach,
With the whole quality wherefore. I fear

59. **Even in the soul of:** i.e., as truly as befits.

67. **Not palating the taste:** failing to distinguish the true flavor.

70. **flat tamed piece:** cask of wine that has been pierced and become flat as a result. "Tame" is the aphetic form of "attame," meaning to broach or pierce.

73. **poised:** balanced.

74. **he as he:** each equal to the other.

78. **scruple:** originally an apothecary's weight; a very small amount.

We shall be much unwelcome.   50
    Aen.   That I assure you.
Troilus had rather Troy were borne to Greece
Than Cressid borne from Troy.
    Par.   There is no help:
The bitter disposition of the time   55
Will have it so. On, lord, we'll follow you.
    Aen. Good morrow, all.   *Exit [with Servant].*
    Par. And tell me, noble Diomed, faith, tell me true,
Even in the soul of sound good fellowship,
Who, in your thoughts, merits fair Helen most,   60
Myself or Menelaus?
    Dio.   Both alike.
He merits well to have her that doth seek her,
Not making any scruple of her soilure,
With such a hell of pain and world of charge;   65
And you as well to keep her that defend her,
Not palating the taste of her dishonor,
With such a costly loss of wealth and friends.
He, like a puling cuckold, would drink up
The lees and dregs of a flat tamed piece;   70
You, like a lecher, out of whorish loins
Are pleased to breed out your inheritors.
Both merits poised, each weighs nor less nor more,
But he as he, the heavier for a whore.
    Par. You are too bitter to your countrywoman.   75
    Dio. She's bitter to her country. Hear me, Paris:
For every false drop in her bawdy veins
A Grecian's life hath sunk; for every scruple
Of her contaminated carrion weight
A Trojan hath been slain. Since she could speak,   80

83. **chapmen:** merchants.

86. **We'll not commend what we intend to sell:** i.e., the Trojans intend to make the Greeks pay dearly for Helen (in lives) if they are to regain her.

⸻⸻⸻⸻⸻⸻⸻⸻⸻⸻⸻

[IV.ii.] As Troilus prepares to leave Cressida, who is petulant at his early morning departure, Aeneas comes seeking him with the news that Cressida is to be handed over to the Greeks. Troilus is stunned but quickly leaves with Aeneas. Cressida tells Pandarus that she will not leave Troilus.

⸻⸻⸻⸻⸻⸻⸻

7. **give as soft attachment to thy senses:** exert as gentle mastery of your consciousness.

She hath not given so many good words breath
As for her Greeks and Trojans suffered death.
  Par. Fair Diomed, you do as chapmen do,
Dispraise the thing that you desire to buy.
But we in silence hold this virtue well: 85
We'll not commend what we intend to sell.
Here lies our way.

                                        Exeunt.

[Scene II. The same. Court of Pandarus' house.]

              Enter Troilus and Cressida.

  Tro. Dear, trouble not yourself: the morn is cold.
  Cres. Then, sweet my lord, I'll call mine uncle
      down:
He shall unbolt the gates.
  Tro.   Trouble him not: 5
To bed, to bed. Sleep kill those pretty eyes
And give as soft attachment to thy senses
As infants' empty of all thought!
  Cres.   Good morrow, then.
  Tro. I prithee now, to bed.   10
  Cres.   Are you aweary of me?
  Tro. O Cressida! but that the busy day,
Waked by the lark, hath roused the ribald crows,
And dreaming night will hide our joys no longer,
I would not from thee.   15
  Cres.   Night hath been too brief.

17. **venomous wights:** malicious creatures.
20. **momentary-swift:** flying with the speed of a moment.
41. **capocchia:** ninny (Italian).
43. **bugbear:** bogey; hobgoblin.

Tro. Beshrew the witch! with venomous wights she
    stays
As tediously as hell but flies the grasps of love
With wings more momentary-swift than thought.   20
You will catch cold and curse me.
    Cres.   Prithee, tarry.
You men will never tarry.
O foolish Cressid! I might have still held off,
And then you would have tarried. Hark! there's one 25
    up.
    Pan. [*Within*] What! 's all the doors open here?
    Tro. It is your uncle.
    Cres. A pestilence on him! Now will he be mocking.
I shall have such a life!   30

Enter Pandarus.

    Pan. How now, how now! How go maidenheads?
Here, you maid! Where's my cousin Cressid?
    Cres. Go hang yourself, you naughty, mocking
    uncle!
You bring me to do—and then you flout me too. 35
    Pan. To do what? To do what? Let her say what.
What have I brought you to do?
    Cres. Come, come, beshrew your heart; You'll ne'er
    be good,
Nor suffer others.   40
    Pan. Ha, ha! Alas, poor wretch! a poor *capocchia!*
Hast not slept tonight? Would he not, a naughty man,
let it sleep? A bugbear take him!

62. **doth import him much:** is of great importance to him.

Cres. Did not I tell you? Would he were knocked
   i' the head!   *One knocks.*   45
Who's that at door? Good uncle, go and see.
My lord, come you again into my chamber.
You smile and mock me, as if I meant naughtily.

Tro. Ha, ha!

Cres. Come, you are deceived, I think of no such   50
   thing.   *Knock.*
How earnestly they knock! Pray you, come in.
I would not for half Troy have you seen here.

                  Exeunt [*Troilus and Cressida*].

Pan. Who's there? What's the matter? Will you beat
down the door? How now! What's the matter?   55

[*Enter Aeneas.*]

Aen. Good morrow, lord, good morrow.

Pan. Who's there? My Lord Aeneas! By my troth, I
knew you not. What news with you so early?

Aen. Is not Prince Troilus here?

Pan. Here! What should he do here?   60

Aen. Come, he is here, my lord: do not deny him.
It doth import him much to speak with me.

Pan. Is he here, say you? 'Tis more than I know, I'll
be sworn. For my own part, I came in late. What
should he do here?   65

Aen. Who? Nay, then. Come, come, you'll do him
wrong ere you are ware. You'll be so true to him, to
be false to him. Do not you know of him, but yet go
fetch him hither. Go.

72. **matter:** business; **rash:** urgent.
79. **concluded:** agreed upon.
80. **state:** statesmen.

Enter Troilus.

Tro. How now! What's the matter?   70
Aen. My lord, I scarce have leisure to salute you,
My matter is so rash. There is at hand
Paris your brother and Deiphobus,
The Grecian Diomed, and our Antenor
Delivered to us; and for him forthwith,   75
Ere the first sacrifice, within this hour,
We must give up to Diomedes' hand
The Lady Cressida.
Tro.   Is it so concluded?
Aen. By Priam and the general state of Troy.   80
They are at hand and ready to effect it.
Tro. How my achievements mock me!
I will go meet them. And, my Lord Aeneas,
We met by chance: you did not find me here.
Aen. Good, good, my lord; the secrets of nature   85
Have not more gift in taciturnity.
                Exeunt [*Troilus and Aeneas*].
Pan. Is't possible? No sooner got but lost! The Devil
take Antenor! The young Prince will go mad. A
plague upon Antenor! I would they had broke 's neck!

[*Enter Cressida.*]

Cres. How now! What's the matter? Who was here?   90
Pan. Ah, ah!
Cres. Why sigh you so profoundly? Where's my
lord? Gone? Tell me, sweet uncle, what's the matter?

103. **changed:** exchanged.
105. **bane:** destruction.

Pan. Would I were as deep under the earth as I am
above!   95

Cres. O the gods! What's the matter?

Pan. Prithee, get thee in. Would thou hadst ne'er
been born! I knew you wouldst be his death. Oh, poor
gentleman! A plague upon Antenor!

Cres. Good uncle, I beseech you, on my knees I 100
beseech you, what's the matter?

Pan. Thou must be gone, wench, thou must be
gone: thou art changed for Antenor. Thou must to
thy father and be gone from Troilus. 'Twill be his
death; 'twill be his bane; he cannot bear it.   105

Cres. O you immortal gods! I will not go.

Pan. Thou must.

Cres. I will not, uncle. I have forgot my father:
I know no touch of consanguinity;
No kin, no love, no blood, no soul so near me   110
As the sweet Troilus. O you gods divine!
Make Cressid's name the very crown of falsehood,
If ever she leave Troilus! Time, force, and death,
Do to this body what extremes you can;
But the strong base and building of my love   115
Is as the very center of the earth,
Drawing all things to it. I'll go in and weep—

Pan. Do, do.

Cres. Tear my bright hair and scratch my praised
  cheeks,   120
Crack my clear voice with sobs, and break my heart
With sounding Troilus. I will not go from Troy.

               Exeunt.

[IV.iii.] Paris, Troilus, Aeneas, Deiphobus, Antenor, and Diomedes arrive at the house of Pandarus, where Troilus is to say farewell to Cressida and turn her over to Diomedes.

1. **great morning:** full daylight.

[IV.iv.] Cressida and Troilus say a tearful goodby; Troilus urges her to be faithful to him. Diomedes brushes aside Troilus' proprietary concern that he treat Cressida well and pledges his service as a tribute to her beauty.

4. **violenteth:** rages.

[Scene III. The same. Street before Pandarus' house.]

Enter Paris, Troilus, Aeneas, Deiphobus, Antenor,
Diomedes.

  Par. It is great morning, and the hour prefixed
For her delivery to this valiant Greek
Comes fast upon. Good my brother Troilus,
Tell you the lady what she is to do
And haste her to the purpose.   5
  Tro.   Walk into her house.
I'll bring her to the Grecian presently.
And to his hand when I deliver her,
Think it an altar and thy brother Troilus
A priest, there off'ring to it his own heart.   [*Exit.*] 10
  Par. I know what 'tis to love;
And would, as I shall pity, I could help!
Please you walk in, my lords.

                                        Exeunt.

[Scene IV. The same. Pandarus' house.]

Enter Pandarus and Cressida.

  Pan. Be moderate, be moderate.
  Cres. Why tell you me of moderation?
The grief is fine, full, perfect, that I taste,
And violenteth in a sense as strong

9. **qualifying:** moderating.
24. **fancy:** love.

As that which causeth it. How can I moderate it?   5
If I could temporize with my affection,
Or brew it to a weak and colder palate,
The like allayment could I give my grief.
My love admits no qualifying dross;
No more my grief, in such a precious loss.   10

Enter Troilus.

Pan. Here, here, here he comes. Ah, sweet ducks!
Cres. O Troilus! Troilus!   *[Embracing him.]*
Pan. What a pair of spectacles is here! Let me em-
brace too. "O heart," as the goodly saying is,
    "Oh heart, heavy heart,   15
      Why sighst thou without breaking?"
where he answers again,
    "Because thou canst not ease thy smart
      By friendship nor by speaking."
There was never a truer rhyme. Let us cast away   20
nothing, for we may live to have need of such a verse.
We see it, we see it. How now, lambs!
Tro. Cressid, I love thee in so strained a purity
That the blest gods, as angry with my fancy,
More bright in zeal than the devotion which   25
Cold lips blow to their deities, take thee from me.
Cres. Have the gods envy?
Pan. Ay, ay, ay, ay. 'Tis too plain a case.
Cres. And is it true that I must go from Troy?
Tro. A hateful truth.   30
Cres.   What, and from Troilus too?

35. **Puts back:** thrusts away.

36. **time of pause:** delay; **beguiles:** cheats.

37. **rejoindure:** joining again.

38. **embrasures:** embracings.

42. **rude brevity and discharge of one:** the brief and uncivil expenditure of one sigh.

44. **Crams his rich thiev'ry up:** stuffs away hurriedly the rich haul he has made.

46. **distinct breath:** separate words.

49. **Distasted:** made distasteful (bitter).

51. **genius:** a man's guiding spirit.

54. **wind:** i.e., windy sighs. Sighing was considered harmful to the heart.

61. **deem:** thought.

Tro. From Troy and Troilus.

Cres.   Is't possible?

Tro. And suddenly, where injury of chance
Puts back leavetaking, justles roughly by   35
All time of pause, rudely beguiles our lips
Of all rejoindure, forcibly prevents
Our locked embrasures, strangles our dear vows
Even in the birth of our own laboring breath.
We two, that with so many thousand sighs   40
Did buy each other, must poorly sell ourselves
With the rude brevity and discharge of one.
Injurious Time now with a robber's haste
Crams his rich thiev'ry up, he knows not how.
As many farewells as be stars in heaven,   45
With distinct breath and consigned kisses to them,
He fumbles up into a loose adieu,
And scants us with a single famished kiss,
Distasted with the salt of broken tears.

Aen. [*Within*] My lord, is the lady ready?   50

Tro. Hark! you are called. Some say the genius so
Cries, "Come!" to him that instantly must die.
Bid them have patience; she shall come anon.

Pan. Where are my tears? Rain, to lay this wind, or
my heart will be blown up by the root.   *Exit.*   55

Cres. I must then to the Grecians?

Tro.   No remedy.

Cres. A woeful Cressid 'mongst the merry Greeks!
When shall we see again?

Tro. Hear me, my love. Be thou but true of heart.   60

Cres. I true! How now! What wicked deem is this?

Tro. Nay, we must use expostulation kindly,

63. **it:** i.e., opportunity to exercise it.

65. **throw my glove to:** challenge.

66. **maculation:** impurity.

67-8. **fashion in/ My sequent protestation:** work in my own vow to follow as a condition.

80. **quality:** good qualities.

82. **arts and exercise:** knowledge of the liberal arts and military skills.

83. **parts with person:** accomplishments combined with personal charm.

84. **godly jealousy:** an echo of II Cor. 11:2: "For I am jealous over you with godly jealousy, and I have espoused you to one husband, that I may present you as a chaste virgin to Christ."

91. **lavolt:** lavolta, a dance featuring high leaps into the air.

93. **prompt and pregnant:** ready.

For it is parting from us.
I speak not "Be thou true," as fearing thee;
For I will throw my glove to Death himself   65
That there's no maculation in thy heart.
But "Be thou true" say I, to fashion in
My sequent protestation. Be thou true,
And I will see thee.

    Cres. Oh, you shall be exposed, my lord, to dangers 70
As infinite as imminent. But I'll be true.

      Tro. And I'll grow friend with danger. Wear this
        sleeve.

      Cres. And you this glove. When shall I see you?

      Tro. I will corrupt the Grecian sentinels,   75
To give thee nightly visitation.
But yet, be true.

      Cres.   O Heavens! "Be true" again!

      Tro. Hear why I speak it, love:
The Grecian youths are full of quality;   80
They're loving, well composed with gifts of nature,
And flowing o'er with arts and exercise.
How novelties may move and parts with person,
Alas, a kind of godly jealousy—
Which, I beseech you, call a virtuous sin—   85
Makes me afeard.

      Cres.   O Heavens! You love me not.

      Tro. Die I a villain then!
In this I do not call your faith in question
So mainly as my merit. I cannot sing,   90
Nor heel the high lavolt, nor sweeten talk,
Nor play at subtle games: fair virtues all,
To which the Grecians are most prompt and pregnant.

95. **still and dumb-discoursive:** silent, but managing to communicate without words.

102. **changeful potency:** unreliable strength.

111. **mere simplicity:** a reputation for sheer honesty (perhaps with the special connotation of ignorance as well).

114. **wit:** wisdom.

118. **port:** gate.

119. **possess:** inform.

120. **Entreat:** treat.

But I can tell that in each grace of these
There lurks a still and dumb-discoursive devil   95
That tempts most cunningly; but be not tempted.
    Cres. Do you think I will?
    Tro. No.
But something may be done that we will not;
And sometimes we are devils to ourselves,   100
When we will tempt the frailty of our powers,
Presuming on their changeful potency.
    Aen. [*Within*] Nay, good my lord!
    Tro.   Come, kiss, and let us part.
    Par. [*Within*] Brother Troilus!   105
    Tro.   Good brother, come you hither;
And bring Aeneas and the Grecian with you.
    Cres. My lord, will you be true?
    Tro. Who, I? Alas, it is my vice, my fault.
Whiles others fish with craft for great opinion,   110
I with great truth catch mere simplicity;
Whilst some with cunning gild their copper crowns,
With truth and plainness I do wear mine bare.
Fear not my truth. The moral of my wit
Is "plain and true": there's all the reach of it.   115

Enter the Greeks [Aeneas, Paris, Antenor, Deiphobus,
                and Diomedes].

Welcome, Sir Diomed! Here is the lady
Which for Antenor we deliver you.
At the port, lord, I'll give her to thy hand;
And by the way possess thee what she is.
Entreat her fair; and, by my soul, fair Greek,   120

125. this prince expects: i.e., that Troilus would claim as exclusively his.

130-31. To shame the seal of my petition to thee/ In praising her: i.e., ignoring Troilus' ardent plea and making Cressida's beauty the basis of his fair treatment of her is a slight to Troilus' honor.

134. even for my charge: for no other reason than that I charge you to do so.

138. moved: angry.

139. place and message: status as a messenger to the enemy.

141. answer to my lust: take responsibility for doing as I please. The specific sense of **lust** as lascivious desire may be intended.

142. To: according to.

146. brave: defiance.

If e'er thou stand at mercy of my sword,
Name Cressid and thy life shall be as safe
As Priam is in Ilion.

 Dio.   Fair Lady Cressid,
So please you, save the thanks this prince expects.   125
The luster in your eye, heaven in your cheek,
Pleads your fair usage; and to Diomed
You shall be mistress and command him wholly.

 Tro. Grecian, thou dost not use me courteously
To shame the seal of my petition to thee   130
In praising her. I tell thee, lord of Greece,
She is as far high-soaring o'er thy praises
As thou unworthy to be called her servant.
I charge thee use her well, even for my charge;
For, by the dreadful Pluto, if thou dost not,   135
Though the great bulk Achilles be thy guard,
I'll cut thy throat.

 Dio.   Oh, be not moved, Prince Troilus.
Let me be privileged by my place and message
To be a speaker free. When I am hence   140
I'll answer to my lust; and know you, lord,
I'll nothing do on charge. To her own worth
She shall be prized; but that you say, "Be't so,"
I speak it in my spirit and honor, "No!"

 Tro. Come, to the port. I'll tell thee, Diomed,   145
This brave shall oft make thee to hide thy head.
Lady, give me your hand; and, as we walk,
To our own selves bend we our needful talk.

     [*Exeunt Troilus, Cressida, and Diomedes.*]
          Sound trumpet.

 Par. Hark! Hector's trumpet.

157. **address:** prepare ourselves.

━━━━━━━━━━━━━━━━━━━━━━━━━━━━━━━━━━━

[**IV.v.**] The foremost Greeks are awaiting Hector's response to Ajax' challenging trumpet when Diomedes appears with Cressida. She consents to kiss each of the generals in turn, and Ulysses comments to Nestor that she is a thorough wanton. Hector appears and, after a brief exchange, declines further combat because of his kinship with Ajax. Greek and Trojan heroes alike exchange compliments with hostile undertones. Troilus asks the way to Calchas' tent, and Ulysses promises to lead him there.

━━━━━━━━━━━━━━━━━━━━━━━

1. **appointment:** equipment.
2. **Anticipating time:** ahead of the time appointed; **With starting courage:** with courage calculated to startle your opponent.
7. **trumpet:** i.e., trumpeter.
9. **sphered bias cheek:** cheek rounded and swelled by blowing.
10. **Aquilon:** the Roman equivalent of Boreas, the north wind.

Aen.   How have we spent this morning!   150
The Prince must think me tardy and remiss,
That swore to ride before him to the field.
    Par. 'Tis Troilus' fault. Come, come, to field with
       him.
    Dei. Let us make ready straight.   155
    Aen. Yea, with a bridegroom's fresh alacrity,
Let us address to tend on Hector's heels.
The glory of our Troy doth this day lie
On his fair worth and single chivalry.

                                        Exeunt.

[Scene V. The Grecian Camp. Lists set out.]

*Enter Ajax, armed; Achilles, Patroclus, Agamemnon,
    Menelaus, Ulysses, Nestor, Calchas, etc.*

    Aga. Here art thou in appointment fresh and fair,
Anticipating time. With starting courage
Give with thy trumpet a loud note to Troy,
Thou dreadful Ajax, that the appalled air
May pierce the head of the great combatant   5
And hale him hither.
    Ajax.   Thou, trumpet, there's my purse.
Now crack thy lungs and split thy brazen pipe.
Blow, villain, till thy sphered bias cheek
Outswell the colic of puffed Aquilon.   10
Come, stretch thy chest, and let thy eyes spout blood:
Thou blowest for Hector.   [*Trumpet sounds.*]

23. **particular:** i.e., not general but bestowed by a single individual.

29. **argument:** subject, or, possibly, cause.

31. **thus:** by kissing; **hardiment:** boldness.

37. **trim:** a fine way to behave.

Achilles. From Guillaume Rouillé, *Promptuarii iconum* (1553).

Uly. No trumpet answers.
Achil.   'Tis but early days.
Aga. Is not yond Diomed, with Calchas' daughter?   15
Uly. 'Tis he, I ken the manner of his gait:
He rises on the toe. That spirit of his
In aspiration lifts him from the earth.

[*Enter Diomedes, with Cressida.*]

Aga. Is this the Lady Cressid?
Dio.   Even she.   20
Aga. Most dearly welcome to the Greeks, sweet lady.
Nes. Our general doth salute you with a kiss.
Uly. Yet is the kindness but particular:
'Twere better she were kissed in general.
Nes. And very courtly counsel. I'll begin.   25
So much for Nestor.
Achil. I'll take that winter from your lips, fair lady.
Achilles bids you welcome.
Men. I had good argument for kissing once.
Patr. But that's no argument for kissing now;   30
For thus popped Paris in his hardiment,
And parted thus you and your argument.
Uly. Oh, deadly gall, and theme of all our scorns!
For which we lose our heads to gild his horns.
Patr. The first was Menelaus' kiss, this, mine: 35
Patroclus kisses you.
Men.   Oh, this is trim!
Patr. Paris and I kiss evermore for him.
Men. I'll have my kiss, sir. Lady, by your leave.
Cres. In kissing, do you render or receive?   40

42. **make my match to live:** stake my life.

45. **boot:** profit.

46. **odd:** singular; unmated.

50. **fillip me o' the head:** i.e., rap his cuckold's horns.

66. **joint and motive:** moving joint.

67. **encounterers:** persons with "come-hither" ways.

68. **give a coasting welcome ere it comes:** meet advances halfway.

70. **ticklish:** lascivious.

Men. Both take and give.

Cres.   I'll make my match to live,
The kiss you take is better than you give:
Therefore no kiss.

Men. I'll give you boot; I'll give you three for one.   45

Cres. You are an odd man: give even, or give none.

Men. An odd man, lady! Every man is odd.

Cres. No, Paris is not; for, you know, 'tis true,
That you are odd and he is even with you.

Men. You fillip me o' the head.   50

Cres.   No, I'll be sworn.

Uly. It were no match, your nail against his horn.
May I, sweet lady, beg a kiss of you?

Cres. You may.

Uly.   I do desire it.   55

Cres.   Why, beg then!

Uly. Why then, for Venus' sake, give me a kiss—
When Helen is a maid again and his.

Cres. I am your debtor: claim it when 'tis due.

Uly. Never's my day, and then a kiss of you.   60

Dio. Lady, a word: I'll bring you to your father.
                        [*Exit with Cressida.*]

Nes. A woman of quick sense.

Uly.   Fie, fie upon her!
There's language in her eye, her cheek, her lip,
Nay, her foot speaks. Her wanton spirits look out   65
At every joint and motive of her body.
Oh, these encounterers, so glib of tongue,
That give a coasting welcome ere it comes
And wide unclasp the tables of their thoughts
To every ticklish reader! set them down   70

71. **spoils of opportunity:** the prey of all comers.

72. **daughters of the game:** harlots.

75-6. **What shall be done/ To him that victory commands?:** how shall the victor be honored?

77. **known:** determined by combat.

78. **the edge of all extremity:** i.e., death.

84. **securely:** overconfidently.

89. **If not Achilles, nothing:** this is possibly an echo of the motto of Cesare Borgia: *Aut Caesar, aut nihil* ("Either Caesar, or nothing").

91-2. **In the extremity of great and little/ Valor and pride excel themselves in Hector:** Hector surpasses others both in the greatness of his valor and in his lack of pride.

For sluttish spoils of opportunity,
And daughters of the game.   [*Trumpet within.*]
  All. The Trojans' trumpet.
  Aga.   Yonder comes the troop.

Flourish. Enter Hector, [armed;] Paris, Aeneas,
  Helenus, Troilus, and [other Trojans, with]
          Attendants.

  Aen. Hail, all the state of Greece! What shall be done   75
To him that victory commands? Or do you purpose
A victor shall be known? Will you the knights
Shall to the edge of all extremity
Pursue each other, or shall they be divided
By any voice or order of the field?   80
Hector bade ask.
  Aga.   Which way would Hector have it?
  Aen. He cares not: he'll obey conditions.
  Achil. 'Tis done like Hector; but securely done,
A little proudly, and great deal misprizing   85
The knight opposed.
  Aen.   If not Achilles, sir,
What is your name?
  Achil.   If not Achilles, nothing.
  Aen. Therefore Achilles. But, whate'er, know this: 90
In the extremity of great and little,
Valor and pride excel themselves in Hector,
The one almost as infinite as all,
The other blank as nothing. Weigh him well,
And that which looks like pride is courtesy.   95

96. **Ajax is half made of Hector's blood:** see I. [ii.] 17 and below, line 136.

100. **maiden:** bloodless.

105. **breath:** mere exercise.

108. **heavy:** sad.

116. **impare:** unsuitable, probably from the Latin *impar*.

118. **subscribes:** yields.

120. **vindicative:** vindictive.

Hector and Ajax. From Geoffrey Whitney, *A Choice of Emblems* (1586).

98

This Ajax is half made of Hector's blood;
In love whereof, half Hector stays at home;
Half heart, half hand, half Hector comes to seek
This blended knight, half Trojan and half Greek.
    Achil. A maiden battle then? Oh, I perceive you.   100

[*Enter Diomedes.*]

    Aga. Here is Sir Diomed. Go, gentle knight,
Stand by our Ajax. As you and Lord Aeneas
Consent upon the order of their fight,
So be it; either to the uttermost,
Or else a breath. The combatants being kin   105
Half stints their strife before their strokes begin.
               [*Ajax and Hector enter the lists.*]
    Uly. They are opposed already.
    Aga. What Trojan is that same that looks so heavy?
    Uly. The youngest son of Priam, a true knight,
Not yet mature, yet matchless, firm of word,   110
Speaking in deeds and deedless in his tongue,
Not soon provoked nor being provoked soon calmed,
His heart and hand both open and both free;
For what he has he gives, what thinks he shows;
Yet gives he not till judgment guide his bounty,   115
Nor dignifies an impare thought with breath:
Manly as Hector, but more dangerous;
For Hector in his blaze of wrath subscribes
To tender objects, but he in heat of action
Is more vindicative than jealous love.   120
They call him Troilus, and on him erect
A second hope, as fairly built as Hector.

124. **Even to his inches:** precisely; **with private soul:** in confidence.

137. **cousin-german:** first cousin.

144. **dexter:** right; **sinister:** left.

150. **mortal:** deadly.

Thus says Aeneas, one that knows the youth
Even to his inches, and with private soul
Did in great Ilion thus translate him to me.   125
                    Alarum. [Hector and Ajax fight.]
　Aga. They are in action.
　Nes. Now, Ajax, hold thine own!
　Tro.   Hector, thou sleepst!
Awake thee!
　Aga. His blows are well disposed. There, Ajax!   130
　Dio. You must no more.   *Trumpets cease.*
　Aen.   Princes, enough, so please you.
　Ajax. I am not warm yet: let us fight again.
　Dio. As Hector pleases.
　Hec.   Why, then will I no more. 135
Thou art, great lord, my father's sister's son,
A cousin-german to great Priam's seed.
The obligation of our blood forbids
A gory emulation 'twixt us twain..
Were thy commixtion Greek and Trojan so   140
That thou couldst say, "This hand is Grecian all,
And this is Trojan; the sinews of this leg
All Greek, and this all Troy; my mother's blood
Runs on the dexter cheek, and this sinister
Bounds in my father's"; by Jove multipotent,   145
Thou shouldst not bear from me a Greekish member
Wherein my sword had not impressure made
Of our rank feud: but the just gods gainsay
That any drop thou borrowedst from thy mother,
My sacred aunt, should by my mortal sword   150
Be drained! Let me embrace thee, Ajax.
By him that thunders, thou hast lusty arms:

156. **free:** generous.

159. **Neoptolemus:** usually known as Pyrrhus, Achillés' son; **mirable:** remarkable.

166. **issue is embracement:** outcome is an embrace.

168. **As seld I have the chance:** elliptical for "which entreatie's I make the more readily, since I seldom have the chance of meeting Hector."

174. **expecters of our Trojan part:** those of the Trojan party who await news of the combat.

Fame. From Henry Peacham, *Minerva Britanna* (1618).

Hector would have them fall upon him thus.
Cousin, all honor to thee!

   Ajax.   I thank thee, Hector.   155
Thou art too gentle and too free a man.
I came to kill thee, cousin, and bear hence
A great addition earned in thy death.

   Hec. Not Neoptolemus so mirable,
On whose bright crest Fame with her loud'st Oyes   160
Cries, "This is he," could promise to himself
A thought of added honor torn from Hector.

   Aen. There is expectance here from both the sides
What further you will do.

   Hec.   We'll answer it: 165
The issue is embracement. Ajax, farewell.

   Ajax. If I might in entreaties find success—
As seld I have the chance—I would desire
My famous cousin to our Grecian tents.

   Dio. 'Tis Agamemnon's wish; and great Achilles   170
Doth long to see unarmed the valiant Hector.

   Hec. Aeneas, call my brother Troilus to me;
And signify this loving interview
To the expecters of our Trojan part.
Desire them home. Give me thy hand, my cousin: 175
I will go eat with thee and see your knights.

       Agamemnon and the rest [*of the Greeks
              come forward*].

   Ajax. Great Agamemnon comes to meet us here.

   Hec. The worthiest of them tell me name by name;
But for Achilles, my own searching eyes

180. **portly:** stately.

187. **Strained purely from all hollow bias-drawing:** utterly purified of all partiality that would render welcome insincere.

190. **imperious:** imperial.

198. **Mars his:** Mars's.

200. **untraded:** uncommon; original.

201. **quondam:** former; **still:** ever.

206. **Laboring for destiny:** dealing out fate to men.

209. **Perseus:** see I. [iii.] 42.

210. **forfeits and subduements:** captives and conquests.

Mars. From Abu Ma'shar, *Albumasar de magnis iunctionis* (1515).

Shall find him by his large and portly size.   180
  Aga. Worthy all arms! as welcome as to one
That would be rid of such an enemy;
But that's no welcome. Understand more clear,
What's past and what's to come is strewed with husks
And formless ruin of oblivion;   185
But in this extant moment faith and troth,
Strained purely from all hollow bias-drawing,
Bids thee, with most divine integrity,
From heart of very heart, great Hector, welcome.
  Hec. I thank thee, most imperious Agamemnon.   190
  Aga. [*To Troilus*] My well-famed lord of Troy, no
    less to you.
  Men. Let me confirm my princely brother's greet-
    ing:
You brace of warlike brothers, welcome hither.   195
  Hec. Who must we answer?
  Aen.   The noble Menelaus.
  Hec. Oh, you, my lord! By Mars his gauntlet,
    thanks!
Mock not, that I affect the untraded oath: 200
Your quondam wife swears still by Venus' glove.
She's well, but bade me not commend her to you.
  Men. Name her not now, sir: she's a deadly theme.
  Hec. Oh, pardon: I offend.
  Nes. I have, thou gallant Trojan, seen thee oft,   205
Laboring for destiny, make cruel way
Through ranks of Greekish youth; and I have seen
    thee,
As hot as Perseus, spur thy Phrygian steed,
Despising many forfeits and subduements,   210

211. **advanced:** raised.

212. **decline:** fall; **declined:** fallen.

218. **still locked in steel:** ever enclosed in a steel helmet.

237. **favor:** face.

The winged horse, Pegasus. From Andrea Alciati, *Emblemata* (1584).
(See I.[iii.]42 and [IV.v.]209.)

When thou hast hung thy advanced sword i' the air,
Not letting it decline on the declined,
That I have said to some my standers-by,
"Lo, Jupiter is yonder, dealing life!"
And I have seen thee pause and take thy breath,   215
When that a ring of Greeks have hemmed thee in,
Like an Olympian wrestling. This have I seen;
But this thy countenance, still locked in steel,
I never saw till now. I knew thy grandsire,
And once fought with him. He was a soldier good;   220
But, by great Mars, the captain of us all,
Never like thee. Let an old man embrace thee;
And, worthy warrior, welcome to our tents.
   Aen. 'Tis the old Nestor.
   Hec. Let me embrace thee, good old chronicle,   225
That hast so long walked hand in hand with Time:
Most reverend Nestor, I am glad to clasp thee.
   Nes. I would my arms could match thee in conten-
     tion,
As they contend with thee in courtesy.   230
   Hec. I would they could.
   Nes. Ha!
By this white beard, I'd fight with thee tomorrow:
Well, welcome, welcome! I have seen the time—
   Uly. I wonder now how yonder city stands   235
When we have here her base and pillar by us.
   Hec. I know your favor, Lord Ulysses, well.
Ah, sir, there's many a Greek and Trojan dead
Since first I saw yourself and Diomed
In Ilion, on your Greekish embassy.   240
   Uly. Sir, I foretold you then what would ensue.

249. The end crowns all: proverbial; compare [III. ii.] 88-9.

259. quoted: noted.

267. read me o'er: i.e., to learn how to master him.

My prophecy is but half his journey yet;
For yonder walls, that pertly front your town,
Yon towers, whose wanton tops do buss the clouds,
Must kiss their own feet.   245

   Hec.   I must not believe you.
There they stand yet: and modestly I think,
The fall of every Phrygian stone will cost
A drop of Grecian blood. The end crowns all,
And that old common arbitrator, Time,   250
Will one day end it.

   Uly.   So to him we leave it.
Most gentle and most valiant Hector, welcome.
After the general, I beseech you next
To feast with me and see me at my tent.   255

   Achil. I shall forestall thee, Lord Ulysses, thou!
Now, Hector, I have fed mine eyes on thee:
I have with exact view perused thee, Hector,
And quoted joint by joint.

   Hec.   Is this Achilles?   260

   Achil. I am Achilles.

   Hec. Stand fair, I pray thee. Let me look on thee.

   Achil. Behold thy fill.

   Hec.   Nay, I have done already.

   Achil. Thou art too brief. I will the second time,   265
As I would buy thee, view thee limb by limb.

   Hec. Oh, like a book of sport thou'lt read me o'er;
But there's more in me than thou understandst.
Why dost thou so oppress me with thine eye?

   Achil. Tell me, you Heavens, in which part of his   270
     body
Shall I destroy him? whether there, or there, or there?

278. **pleasantly:** easily, rather than by painful effort.

279. **prenominate:** name beforehand; **nice:** precise.

285. **forge:** the forge of Vulcan; **stithied:** forged.

295. **stomach:** (1) appetite; (2) courage; **general state:** whole body of Greek statesmen.

296. **odd:** at odds.

298. **pelting:** paltry; contemptible.

301. **fell:** fierce; savage.

303. **match:** bargain.

Vulcan overseeing the work of his forge. From Vincenzo Cartari, *Imagini delli dei de gli antichi* (1674).

That I may give the local wound a name,
And make distinct the very breach whereout
Hector's great spirit flew. Answer me, Heavens!   275
   Hec. It would discredit the blest gods, proud man,
To answer such a question. Stand again!
Thinkst thou to catch my life so pleasantly
As to prenominate in nice conjecture
Where thou wilt hit me dead?   280
   Achil.   I tell thee, yea.
   Hec. Wert thou an oracle to tell me so,
I'd not believe thee. Henceforth guard thee well;
For I'll not kill thee there, nor there, nor there;
But, by the forge that stithied Mars his helm,   285
I'll kill thee everywhere, yea, o'er and o'er.
You wisest Grecians, pardon me this brag:
His insolence draws folly from my lips;
But I'll endeavor deeds to match these words,
Or may I never—   290
   Ajax.   Do not chafe thee, cousin.
And you, Achilles, let these threats alone
Till accident or purpose brings you to't.
You may have every day enough of Hector,
If you have stomach. The general state, I fear,   295
Can scarce entreat you to be odd with him.
   Hec. I pray you, let us see you in the field.
We have had pelting wars since you refused
The Grecians' cause.
   Achil.   Dost thou entreat me, Hector?   300
Tomorrow do I meet thee, fell as death:
Tonight all friends.
   Hec.   Thy hand upon that match.

305. in the full convive we: let us all feast together.

307. severally entreat him: deal with him individually.

311. keep: reside.

315. gives all gaze and bent of amorous view: fully bends his amorous glance.

321. gentle: gently; courteously.

324-25. to such as boasting show their scars,/ A mock is due: i.e., the soldier is mocked if he shows pride in his battle scars; Troilus would deserve equal scorn if he revealed the pain caused him by his love for Cressida.

Aga. First, all you peers of Greece, go to my tent:
There in the full convive we. Afterward,   305
As Hector's leisure and your bounties shall
Concur together, severally entreat him.
Beat loud the taborines, let the trumpets blow,
That this great soldier may his welcome know.

        Exeunt [all but Troilus and Ulysses].

  Tro. My Lord Ulysses, tell me, I beseech you,   310
In what place of the field doth Calchas keep?

  Uly. At Menelaus' tent, most princely Troilus.
There Diomed doth feast with him tonight,
Who neither looks upon the heaven nor earth
But gives all gaze and bent of amorous view   315
On the fair Cressid.

  Tro. Shall I, sweet lord, be bound to you so much,
After we part from Agamemnon's tent,
To bring me thither?

  Uly.   You shall command me, sir. 320
As gentle tell me, of what honor was
This Cressida in Troy? Had she no lover there
That wails her absence?

  Tro. Oh, sir, to such as boasting show their scars,
A mock is due. Will you walk on, my lord?   325
She was beloved, she loved; she is, and doth:
But still sweet love is food for Fortune's tooth.

                Exeunt.

TROILUS
AND
CRESSIDA

ACT V

[V.i.] While Achilles awaits Hector, who is to dine in his tent, Thersites delivers a message from Hecuba with a token enclosed from Polyxena, reminding him of his pledge to refrain from the fight. The other Trojan leaders are to be feasted by the Greeks, and Troilus and Ulysses follow Diomedes to the tent of Calchas.

▬▬▬▬▬▬▬▬▬▬▬▬▬

13. **The surgeon's box, or the patient's wound:** Thersites puns on another meaning of **tent:** a surgeon's probe; see [II. ii.] 16.

14. **Well said, adversity:** i.e., a good answer, since it enables Thersites to maintain his adverse position by ignoring the real point of Patroclus' words.

[ACT V]

[Scene I. The Grecian Camp. Before Achilles' tent.]

Enter Achilles and Patroclus.

Achil. I'll heat his blood with Greekish wine to-
night,
Which with my scimitar I'll cool tomorrow.
Patroclus, let us feast him to the height.
   Patr. Here comes Thersites.   5

Enter Thersites.

Achil.   How now, thou core of envy!
Thou crusty batch of nature, what's the news?
   Ther. Why, thou picture of what thou seemst and
idol of idiot-worshipers, here's a letter for thee.
   Achil. From whence, fragment?   10
   Ther. Why, thou full dish of fool, from Troy.
   Patr. Who keeps the tent now?
   Ther. The surgeon's box, or the patient's wound.
   Patr. Well said, adversity! and what need these
tricks?   15
   Ther. Prithee, be silent, boy: I profit not by thy
talk. Thou art said to be Achilles' male varlet.

21. **gravel i' the back:** kidney stones; **lethargies:** apoplexies.

23. **imposthume:** abscesses; **limekilns:** burnings; i.e., psoriasis (?).

24. **riveled:** shriveled.

24-5. **fee simple of the tetter:** permanent skin eruption.

25-6. **preposterous discoveries:** perverse inventions; referring to "masculine whores."

30. **ruinous butt:** ruined cask.

30-1. **indistinguishable:** shapeless.

33. **immaterial:** insubstantial; **sleave silk:** floss silk; **sarcenet:** a fine (flimsy) silk.

36. **water flies:** showy and insubstantial idlers; **diminutives of Nature:** i.e., creatures who reflect unfavorably on Nature's creative powers and thus diminish her.

Patr. Male varlet, you rogue! What's that?

Ther. Why, his masculine whore. Now, the rotten
diseases of the South, the guts-griping ruptures, ca- 20
tarrhs, loads o' gravel i' the back, lethargies, cold
palsies, raw eyes, dirt-rotten livers, wheezing lungs,
bladders full of imposthume, sciaticas, limekilns i'
the palm, incurable boneache, and the riveled fee
simple of the tetter, take and take again such pre- 25
posterous discoveries!

Patr. Why, thou damnable box of envy, thou, what
meanst thou to curse thus?

Ther. Do I curse thee?

Patr. Why, no, you ruinous butt, you whoreson in- 30
distinguishable cur, no.

Ther. No! why art thou then exasperate, thou idle
immaterial skein of sleave silk, thou green sarcenet
flap for a sore eye, thou tassel of a prodigal's purse,
thou? Ah, how the poor world is pestered with such 35
water flies, diminutives of Nature!

Patr. Out, gall!

Ther. Finch egg!

Achil. My sweet Patroclus, I am thwarted quite
From my great purpose in tomorrow's battle. 40
Here is a letter from Queen Hecuba,
A token from her daughter, my fair love,
Both taxing me and gaging me to keep
An oath that I have sworn. I will not break it.
Fall Greeks, fail fame, honor or go or stay: 45
My major vow lies here; this I'll obey.
Come, come, Thersites, help to trim my tent.
This night in banqueting must all be spent.

54. **quails:** harlots.

56. **Jupiter . . . the bull:** referring to Jupiter's transformation to a bull to abduct Europa; **primitive:** first.

57. **oblique memorial of cuckolds:** indirect symbol of the cuckold, because both are horned; **thrifty:** miserly.

58. **shoeing-horn:** tool.

59-60. **larded . . . forced:** stuffed.

63. **fitchew:** polecat.

64. **puttock:** kite, a scavenging bird.

67. **lazar:** leper.

68. **so:** so long as.

Away, Patroclus!   *Exeunt [Achilles and Patroclus].*

   Ther. With too much blood and too little brain,   50
these two may run mad; but, if with too much brain
and too little blood they do, I'll be a curer of madmen. Here's Agamemnon, an honest fellow enough
and one that loves quails; but he has not so much
brain as earwax; and the goodly transformation of   55
Jupiter there, his brother, the bull, the primitive
statue and oblique memorial of cuckolds, a thrifty
shoeing-horn in a chain, hanging at his brother's leg
—to what form but that he is should wit larded with
malice and malice forced with wit turn him to? To   60
an ass were nothing: he is both ass and ox. To an ox
were nothing: he is both ox and ass. To be a dog, a
mule, a cat, a fitchew, a toad, a lizard, an owl, a
puttock, or a herring without a roe, I would not care;
but to be Menelaus! I would conspire against Des-   65
tiny. Ask me not what I would be if I were not
Thersites; for I care not to be the louse of a lazar,
so I were not Menelaus. Heyday! sprites and fires!

Enter Hector, [Troilus,] Ajax, Agamemnon, Ulysses,
  Nestor, [Menelaus,] and Diomedes, with lights.

   Aga. We go wrong, we go wrong.
   Ajax.   No, yonder 'tis,   70
There, where we see the lights.
   Hec.   I trouble you.
   Ajax. No, not a whit.

82. **draught:** privy.

Menelaus. From Guillaume Rouillé, *Promptuarii iconum* (1553).

Enter Achilles.

Uly.   Here comes himself to guide you.
Achil. Welcome, brave Hector. Welcome, princes   75
    all.
Aga. So now, fair Prince of Troy, I bid good night.
Ajax commands the guard to tend on you.
Hec. Thanks and good night to the Greeks' general.
Men. Good night, my lord.   80
Hec.   Good night, sweet Lord Menelaus.
Ther. Sweet draught! "Sweet," quoth a! Sweet sink,
sweet sewer!
Achil. Good night and welcome, both at once, to
    those   85
That go or tarry.
Aga. Good night.   *Exeunt Agamemnon, Menelaus.*
Achil. Old Nestor tarries; and you too, Diomed,
Keep Hector company an hour or two.
Dio. I cannot, lord: I have important business,   90
The tide whereof is now. Good night, great Hector.
Hec. Give me your hand.
Uly. [*Aside to Troilus*] Follow his torch: he goes
    to Calchas' tent.
I'll keep you company.   95
Tro.   Sweet sir, you honor me.
Hec. And so, good night.
    [*Exit Diomedes, Ulysses and Troilus following.*]
Achil. Come, come, enter my tent.
        Exeunt [Achilles, Hector, Ajax, and Nestor].
Ther. That same Diomed's a false-hearted rogue, a

100. **unjust:** dishonest.
106. **leave:** fail.

━━━━━━━━━━━━━━━━━━━━━━━━━━━━━━━━━━━

[**V.ii.**] In front of Calchas' tent Ulysses, Troilus, and Thersites witness a meeting between Diomedes and Cressida, in which it is evident that Troilus' mistress has agreed to an assignation. She even gives the Greek the sleeve that had been Troilus' pledge of fidelity. Troilus, stunned by this evidence of Cressida's faithlessness, refuses to accept what he knows to be true, that it was indeed Cressida whom he saw acting as coyly with Diomedes as she had once behaved with him. He vows to challenge Diomedes when he wears the sleeve on his helmet.

━━━━━━━━━━━━━━━━━━━━━

6. **discover:** reveal.

most unjust knave. I will no more trust him when he 100
leers than I will a serpent when he hisses. He will
spend his mouth and promise like Brabbler the
hound; but when he performs, astronomers foretell
it: it is prodigious, there will come some change. The
sun borrows of the moon when Diomed keeps his 105
word. I will rather leave to see Hector than not to
dog him. They say he keeps a Trojan drab and uses
the traitor Calchas' tent. I'll after. Nothing but
lechery! All incontinent varlets!

                                          Exit.

[Scene II. The same. Before Calchas' tent.]

Enter Diomedes.

Dio. What, are you up here, ho? Speak.
Cal. [*Within*] Who calls?
Dio. Diomed. Calchas, I think. Where's your daugh-
ter?
Cal. [*Within*] She comes to you.   5

Enter Troilus and Ulysses, [at a distance; after them,
Thersites].

Uly. Stand where the torch may not discover us.

Enter Cressida.

Tro. Cressid comes forth to him.
Dio.   How now, my charge!

12. **sing:** i.e., know by heart.
14. **cliff:** (1) clef; key; (2) cleft.
26. **tell a pin:** i.e., don't bother.

Cres. Now, my sweet guardian! Hark, a word with
   you.   [*Whispers.*]   10

Tro. Yea, so familiar!

Uly. She will sing any man at first sight.

Ther. And any man may sing her, if he can take
her cliff: she's noted.

Dio. Will you remember?   15

Cres. Remember! Yes.

Dio. Nay, but do, then;
And let your mind be coupled with your words.

Tro. What shall she remember?

Uly. List.   20

Cres. Sweet honey Greek, tempt me no more to
   folly.

Ther. Roguery!

Dio. Nay, then—

Cres. I'll tell you what—   25

Dio. Foh, foh! Come, tell a pin. You are forsworn.

Cres. In faith, I cannot. What would you have me
   do?

Ther. A juggling trick—to be secretly open.

Dio. What did you swear you would bestow on me?   30

Cres. I prithee, do not hold me to mine oath:
Bid me do anything but that, sweet Greek.

Dio. Good night.

Tro. Hold, patience!

Uly. How now, Trojan!   35

Cres. Diomed—

Dio. No, no, good night. I'll be your fool no more.

Tro. Thy better must.

Cres. Hark, a word in your ear.

Tro. O plague and madness!   40
Uly. You are moved, Prince. Let us depart, I pray,
Lest your displeasure should enlarge itself
To wrathful terms. This place is dangerous,
The time right deadly. I beseech you, go.
    Tro. Behold, I pray you!   45
    Uly.   Nay, good my lord, go off.
You flow to great distraction. Come, my lord.
    Tro. I prithee, stay.
    Uly.   You have not patience: come.
    Tro. I pray you, stay. By hell and all hell's tor-   50
      ments,
I will not speak a word.
    Dio.   And so, good night.
    Cres. Nay, but you part in anger.
    Tro.   Doth that grieve thee?   55
Oh, withered truth!
    Uly.   How now, my lord?
    Tro.   By Jove,
I will be patient.
    Cres.   Guardian!—why, Greek!   60
    Dio. Foh, foh! Adieu. You palter.
    Cres. In faith, I do not. Come hither once again.
    Uly. You shake, my lord, at something. Will you
     go?
You will break out.   65
    Tro.   She strokes his cheek!
    Uly.   Come, come.
    Tro. Nay, stay. By Jove, I will not speak a word.
There is between my will and all offenses
A guard of patience. Stay a little while.   70

71. **Luxury:** lechery personified.
72. **potato:** considered an aphrodisiac.
93. **sharpens:** whets Diomedes' appetite.

Ther. How the devil Luxury, with his fat rump and potato finger, tickles these together! Fry, lechery, fry!

Dio. But will you, then?

Cres. In faith, I will, lo: never trust me else.　　75

Dio. Give me some token for the surety of it.

Cres. I'll fetch you one.　　　　　　　*Exit.*

Uly. You have sworn patience.

Tro.　　　　　　　　Fear me not, sweet lord:
I will not be myself, nor have cognition　　80
Of what I feel: I am all patience.

Enter Cressida.

Tro. Now the pledge: now, now, now!

Cres. Here, Diomed, keep this sleeve.

Tro. O beauty! where is thy faith?

Uly.　　　　　　　　My lord—　　85

Tro. I will be patient: outwardly I will.

Cres. You look upon that sleeve: behold it well.
He loved me—O false wench!—Give't me again.

Dio. Whose was't?

Cres. It is no matter, now I ha't again.　　90
I will not meet with you tomorrow night.
I prithee, Diomed, visit me no more.

Ther. Now she sharpens. Well said, whetstone!

Dio. I shall have it.

Cres.　　　　　　　What, this?　　95

Dio.　　　　　　　　Ay, that.

Cres. O all you gods! O pretty, pretty pledge!

100. **memorial:** in token of remembrance.

115. **Diana's waitingwomen:** i.e., the stars, considered as attendants of the moon-goddess, Diana.

127. **straight starts you:** immediately sets you off.

Thy master now lies thinking on his bed
Of thee and me, and sighs, and takes my glove,
And gives memorial dainty kisses to it,   100
As I kiss thee. Nay, do not snatch it from me:
He that takes that doth take my heart withal.
   Dio. I had your heart before: this follows it.
   Tro. I did swear patience.
   Cres. You shall not have it, Diomed, faith, you shall   105
    not.
I'll give you something else.
   Dio. I will have this. Whose was it?
   Cres.   It is no matter.
   Dio. Come, tell me whose it was.   110
   Cres. 'Twas one's that loved me better than you
    will.
But now you have it, take it.
   Dio.   Whose was it?
   Cres. By all Diana's waitingwomen yond,   115
And by herself, I will not tell you whose.
   Dio. Tomorrow will I wear it on my helm
And grieve his spirit that dares not challenge it.
   Tro. Wert thou the Devil, and worest it on thy horn,
It should be challenged.   120
   Cres. Well, well, 'tis done, 'tis past; and yet it is
    not.
I will not keep my word.
   Dio.   Why then, farewell!
Thou never shalt mock Diomed again.   125
   Cres. You shall not go. One cannot speak a word
But it straight starts you.
   Dio.   I do not like this fooling.

129. **likes:** pleases.
141. **proof of strength:** strong proof.

Ther. Nor I, by Pluto; but that that likes not you
Pleases me best.   130
   Dio.   What, shall I come? The hour—
   Cres. Ay, come. O Jove! do come. I shall be plagued.
   Dio. Farewell till then.
   Cres.   Good night. I prithee, come.
                              Exit [*Diomedes*].
Troilus, farewell! one eye yet looks on thee,   135
But with my heart the other eye doth see.
Ah, poor our sex! this fault in us I find,
The error of our eye directs our mind.
What error leads must err: oh, then conclude,
Minds swayed by eyes are full of turpitude.   *Exit.* 140
   Ther. A proof of strength she could not publish
        more
Unless she said, "My mind is now turned whore."
   Uly. All's done, my lord.
   Tro.   It is.   145
   Uly.   Why stay we then?
   Tro. To make a recordation to my soul
Of every syllable that here was spoke.
But if I tell how these two did coact,
Shall I not lie in publishing a truth?   150
Sith yet there is a credence in my heart,
An esperance so obstinately strong
That doth invert the attest of eyes and ears,
As if those organs had deceptious functions,
Created only to calumniate.   155
Was Cressid here?
   Uly.   I cannot conjure, Trojan.

164. **apt:** ready.

164-65. **theme/ For depravation:** subject meriting disparagement.

165. **square:** measure; **general:** whole.

170. **swagger himself out on's own eyes:** i.e., defy the testimony of his own eyes.

175. **rule in unity:** a principle of oneness or indivisibility.

176. **discourse:** reason.

178-80. **where reason can revolt/ Without perdition, and loss assume all reason/ Without revolt:** where reason can be unreasonable without destruction of its basic nature, and unreason (loss) usurp reason's function without being disloyal to it. It is irrational to disbelieve the evidence of his own eyes, but in his irrational state he employs reason as though he were sane.

181. **conduce a fight:** gather together the forces of a battle.

182-86. **a thing inseparate . . . enter:** the indivisible Cressida seems two different women as far apart as the distance between sky and earth, and yet one Cressida shades over into the other so precisely that there is not a hairbreadth between them.

185. **orifex:** opening; **subtle:** fine.

186. **Ariachne:** i.e., Arachne, who challenged Minerva's skill at weaving and had her web broken by the angry goddess, who also changed her to a spider. The spelling **Ariachne** may result from confusion with Ariadne, who led Theseus from the labyrinth by means of a spool of thread.

187. **Instance:** as evidence, there is this.

Tro. She was not, sure.

Uly.   Most sure she was.

Tro. Why, my negation hath no taste of madness.   160

Uly. Nor mine, my lord. Cressid was here but now.

Tro. Let it not be believed for womanhood!
Think, we had mothers: do not give advantage
To stubborn critics, apt, without a theme
For depravation, to square the general sex   165
By Cressid's rule. Rather think this not Cressid.

Uly. What hath she done, Prince, that can soil our
       mothers?

Tro. Nothing at all, unless that this were she.

Ther. Will 'a swagger himself out on's own eyes?   170

Tro. This she? No, this is Diomed's Cressida.
If beauty have a soul, this is not she;
If souls guide vows, if vows be sanctimonies,
If sanctimony be the gods' delight,
If there be rule in unity itself,   175
This is not she. O madness of discourse,
That cause sets up with and against itself!
Bifold authority! where reason can revolt
Without perdition, and loss assume all reason
Without revolt. This is, and is not, Cressid!   180
Within my soul there doth conduce a fight
Of this strange nature, that a thing inseparate
Divides more wider than the sky and earth;
And yet the spacious breadth of this division
Admits no orifex for a point as subtle   185
As Ariachne's broken woof to enter.
Instance, O instance! strong as Pluto's gates:
Cressid is mine, tied with the bonds of Heaven.

192. **knot, five-finger-tied:** bond, pledged by the giving of her hand.

193. **orts:** leftovers.

195. **o'ereaten:** i.e., eaten to excess, so that her stomach has revolted. In other words, Cressida has already had a surfeit of being faithful.

196. **attached:** seized.

207. **hurricano:** waterspout.

208. **Constringed:** constricted.

212. **tickle it:** tickle Diomedes with his sword; **concupy:** lust.

Minerva and Arachne. From Lodovico Dolce, *Le trasformationi* (1558).
(See [V.ii.]186.)

Instance, O instance! strong as Heaven itself:
The bonds of Heaven are slipped, dissolved, and 190
    loosed,
And with another knot, five-finger-tied,
The fractions of her faith, orts of her love,
The fragments, scraps, the bits and greasy relics
Of her o'ereaten faith are bound to Diomed.   195

Uly. May worthy Troilus be half attached
With that which here his passion doth express?

   Tro. Ay, Greek; and that shall be divulged well
In characters as red as Mars his heart
Inflamed with Venus. Never did young man fancy   200
With so eternal and so fixed a soul.
Hark, Greek: as much as I do Cressid love,
So much by weight hate I her Diomed.
That sleeve is mine that he'll bear on his helm.
Were it a casque composed by Vulcan's skill,   205
My sword should bite it. Not the dreadful spout
Which shipmen do the hurricano call,
Constringed in mass by the almighty sun,
Shall dizzy with more clamor Neptune's ear
In his descent than shall my prompted sword   210
Falling on Diomed.

   Ther. He'll tickle it for his concupy.

   Tro. O Cressid! O false Cressid! false, false, false!
Let all untruths stand by thy stained name
And they'll seem glorious.   215

   Uly.   Oh, contain yourself:
Your passion draws ears hither.

223. **revolted:** faithless.

228. **bode:** the raven's croak was proverbially an ill omen.

229-30. **intelligence of:** information about.

231. **commodious:** accommodating.

<hr/>

[V.iii.] Hector's wife, Andromache, vainly seeks to dissuade him from fighting, but he feels that honor requires him to fulfill his oath to the gods. Cassandra's forebodings go equally unheeded. Hector, on his part, tries to persuade Troilus not to fight, but his younger brother, in a ferocious mood, is determined to slaughter Greeks mercilessly. As he prepares for the field, Pandarus enters with a letter from Cressida, which Troilus tears and throws to the wind, convinced that her words are as faithless as her heart.

<hr/>

4. **train:** entice; tempt.

Enter Aeneas.

Aen. I have been seeking you this hour, my lord.
Hector by this is arming him in Troy.
Ajax, your guard, stays to conduct you home.   220
   Tro. Have with you, Prince. My courteous lord,
     adieu.
Farewell, revolted fair! And Diomed,
Stand fast and wear a castle on thy head!
   Uly. I'll bring you to the gates.   225
   Tro. Accept distracted thanks.
       Exeunt Troilus, Aeneas, and Ulysses.
   Ther. Would I could meet that rogue Diomed! I
would croak like a raven, I would bode, I would
bode. Patroclus will give me anything for the intelligence of this whore. The parrot will not do more for 230
an almond than he for a commodious drab. Lechery,
lechery! Still wars and lechery! Nothing else holds
fashion. A burning devil take them!

                           Exit.

[Scene III. Troy. Before Priam's Palace.]

Enter Hector and Andromache.

   And. When was my lord so much ungently tempered,
To stop his ears against admonishment?
Unarm, unarm, and do not fight today.
   Hec. You train me to offend you: Get you in.

11. **dear:** serious.

20. **peevish:** foolish.

24. **hurt by being just:** be honorable at the cost of hurting another.

25. **For:** because.

27. **It is the purpose that makes strong the vow:** i.e., the binding force of a vow is determined by its moral value.

31. **keeps the weather of my fate:** has the advantage of my fate; i.e., my fate is at the mercy of my honor. To "have the weather of" another ship gives a vessel a strategic advantage.

By all the everlasting gods, I'll go!   5
  And. My dreams will, sure, prove ominous to the
    day.
  Hec. No more, I say.

Enter Cassandra.

  Cas.   Where is my brother Hector?
  And. Here, sister, armed, and bloody in intent.   10
Consort with me in loud and dear petition;
Pursue we him on knees; for I have dreamed
Of bloody turbulence, and this whole night
Hath nothing been but shapes and forms of slaughter.
  Cas. Oh, 'tis true.   15
  Hec.   Ho! bid my trumpet sound!
  Cas. No notes of sally, for the Heavens, sweet
    brother.
  Hec. Be gone, I say. The gods have heard me swear.
  Cas. The gods are deaf to hot and peevish vows.   20
They are polluted off'rings, more abhorred
Than spotted livers in the sacrifice.
  And. Oh, be persuaded! Do not count it holy
To hurt by being just. It is as lawful,
For we would give much, to use violent thefts   25
And rob in the behalf of charity.
  Cas. It is the purpose that makes strong the vow;
But vows to every purpose must not hold:
Unarm, sweet Hector.
  Hec.   Hold you still, I say;   30
Mine honor keeps the weather of my fate:

32. dear man: honorable man.

43-4. a vice of mercy . . ./Which better fits a lion than a man: referring to a proverbial idea that the lion spares a suppliant.

54. hermit: i.e., a beadsman, who prays for others.

57. ruthful: exciting compassion; **ruth:** mercy.

Life every man holds dear; but the dear man
Holds honor far more precious-dear than life.

Enter Troilus.

How now, young man! Meanst thou to fight today?

 And. Cassandra, call my father to persuade.   35

          Exit Cassandra.

 Hec. No, faith, young Troilus: doff thy harness,
 youth.
I am today i' the vein of chivalry.
Let grow thy sinews till their knots be strong,
And tempt not yet the brushes of the war.   40
Unarm thee, go: and doubt thou not, brave boy,
I'll stand today for thee and me and Troy.

 Tro. Brother, you have a vice of mercy in you
Which better fits a lion than a man.

 Hec. What vice is that, good Troilus? Chide me for   45
 it.

 Tro. When many times the captive Grecian falls,
Even in the fan and wind of your fair sword,
You bid them rise and live.

 Hec. Oh, 'tis fair play.   50

 Tro.   Fool's play, by Heaven, Hector.

 Hec. How now! how now!

 Tro.   For the love of all the gods,
Let's leave the hermit Pity with our mother;
And when we have our armors buckled on,   55
The venomed vengeance ride upon our swords,
Spur them to ruthful work, rein them from ruth!

59. **then 'tis wars:** such action as I have described is true warfare.

63. **truncheon:** baton of office,. wielded by the arbiter of a combat in the lists.

65. **o'ergalled:** irritated; **recourse:** repeated flow.

70. **stay:** support.

76. **enrapt:** entranced (by a prophetic vision).

80. **engaged:** pledged.

81. **Even in the faith of valor:** by the very honor of a valiant man.

Hec. Fie, savage, fie!

Tro.   Hector, then 'tis wars.

Hec. Troilus, I would not have you fight today.   60

Tro. Who should withhold me?
Not fate, obedience, nor the hand of Mars,
Beck'ning with fiery truncheon my retire;
Not Priamus and Hecuba on knees,
Their eyes o'ergalled with recourse of tears;   65
Nor you, my brother, with your true sword drawn,
Opposed to hinder me, should stop my way,
But by my ruin.

Enter Priam and Cassandra.

Cas. Lay hold upon him, Priam, hold him fast.
He is thy crutch: now if thou lose thy stay,   70
Thou, on him leaning, and all Troy on thee,
Fall all together.

Pri.   Come, Hector, come, go back.
Thy wife hath dreamt; thy mother hath had visions;
Cassandra doth foresee; and I myself   75
Am like a prophet suddenly enrapt
To tell thee that this day is ominous.
Therefore, come back.

Hec.   Aeneas is afield;
And I do stand engaged to many Greeks,   80
Even in the faith of valor, to appear
This morning to them.

Pri.   Ay, but thou shalt not go.

Hec. I must not break my faith.
You know me dutiful: therefore, dear sir,   85

86. shame respect: disgrace the respect due a father from his son.

87. consent and voice: consenting voice; approval.

101. antics: madmen.

104. soft: wait.

Hecuba in Troy's last hours. From Gabriele Simeoni, *La vita et Metamorfoseo d'Ovidio* (1559).

Let me not shame respect, but give me leave
To take that course by your consent and voice
Which you do here forbid me, royal Priam.
 Cas. O Priam, yield not to him!
 And.   Do not, dear father. 90
 Hec. Andromache, I am offended with you.
Upon the love you bear me, get you in.
          Exit Andromache.
 Tro. This foolish, dreaming, superstitious girl
Makes all these bodements.
 Cas.   Oh, farewell, dear Hector! 95
Look how thou diest! Look how thy eye turns pale!
Look how thy wounds do bleed at many vents!
Hark how Troy roars! how Hecuba cries out!
How poor Andromache shrills her dolors forth!
Behold, distraction, frenzy, and amazement,   100
Like witless antics, one another meet,
And all cry, "Hector! Hector's dead! O Hector!"
 Tro. Away! away!
 Cas. Farewell: yet, soft! Hector, I take my leave.
Thou dost thyself and all our Troy deceive.   *Exit.* 105
 Hec. You are amazed, my Liege, at her exclaim.
Go in and cheer the town. We'll forth and fight,
Do deeds worth praise and tell you them at night.
 Pri. Farewell! The gods with safety stand about
  thee!   110
   [*Exeunt, severally, Priam and Hector.*] *Alarum.*
 Tro. They are at it, hark! Proud Diomed, believe,
I come to lose my arm or win my sleeve.

117. **tisick:** phthisic, an affection of the lungs.
127. **Go, wind:** go, breath (words).
128. **words and errors:** lies.

—————————————————————————————

[**V. iv.**] In a field between Troy and the Grecian camp, Troilus encounters Diomedes. Hector challenges Thersites but lets him go when the latter confesses himself a rascal.

—————————————————————————————

1. **clapperclawing:** mauling.

Enter Pandarus.

Pan. Do you hear, my lord? Do you hear?

Tro. What now?

Pan. Here's a letter come from yond poor girl.   115

Tro. Let me read.

Pan. A whoreson tisick, a whoreson rascally tisick
so troubles me, and the foolish fortune of this girl;
and what one thing, what another, that I shall leave
you one o' th's days. And I have a rheum in mine eyes   120
too, and such an ache in my bones that, unless a man
were cursed, I cannot tell what to think on't. What
says she there?

Tro. Words, words, mere words, no matter from the
heart: 125
The effect doth operate another way.

                    [*Tearing the letter.*]
Go, wind, to wind, there turn and change together.
My love with words and errors still she feeds,
But edifies another with her deeds.

                    Exeunt [*severally*].

[Scene IV. Plains between Troy and the Grecian
Camp.]

Alarum. Enter Thersites. Excursions.

Ther. Now they are clapperclawing one another:
I'll go look on. That dissembling, abominable varlet,

8. **of:** on.

8-9. **sleeveless:** useless.

10. **crafty swearing:** swearing in craft what they have no intention of doing.

12. **set me:** set (the ethical dative).

12-3. **in policy:** in cunning; expediently.

16. **proclaim barbarism:** acclaim barbarism, instead of civilized behavior, as the new rule of conduct.

22-3. **advantageous care/ Withdrew me from the odds of multitude:** care for my advantage caused me to withdraw from a multitude where the odds were so against me.

Diomed, has got that same scurvy, doting, foolish
young knave's sleeve of Troy there in his helm. I
would fain see them meet, that that same young   5
Trojan ass, that loves the whore there, might send
that Greekish whoremasterly villain with the sleeve
back to the dissembling, luxurious drab, of a sleeveless errand. O' the t'other side, the policy of those
crafty swearing rascals, that stale old mouse-eaten   10
dry cheese, Nestor, and that same dog-fox, Ulysses,
is not proved worth a blackberry. They set me up in
policy that mongrel cur, Ajax, against that dog of as
bad a kind, Achilles. And now is the cur Ajax prouder
than the cur Achilles and will not arm today; where-   15
upon the Grecians began to proclaim barbarism, and
policy grows into an ill opinion.

Enter Diomedes and Troilus.

Soft! here comes sleeve and t'other.
     Tro. Fly not, for shouldst thou take the river Styx,
I would swim after.   20
     Dio.   Thou dost miscall retire.
I do not fly, but advantageous care
Withdrew me from the odds of multitude.
Have at thee!
     Ther. Hold thy whore, Grecian! Now for thy whore,   25
        Trojan!
Now the sleeve, now the sleeve!
               [*Exeunt Troilus and Diomedes, fighting.*]

30. **blood and honor:** honorable blood.

34. **God-a-mercy:** thank God.

<hr>

[**V.v.**] Diomedes has acquired Troilus' horse, which he gives a servant to deliver to Cressida. The Greeks have had heavy losses, including Patroclus, slain by Hector. The news has aroused the sluggish Achilles, who is arming himself for the field and vowing vengeance. Troilus is reported to have taken a great toll of the enemy in reckless fashion.

<hr>

3. **commend:** offer.

Enter Hector.

Hec. What art thou, Greek? Art thou for Hector's
  match?
Art thou of blood and honor? 30
  Ther. No, no. I am a rascal, a scurvy, railing knave,
a very filthy rogue.
  Hec. I do believe thee. Live.   *[Exit.]*
  Ther. God-a-mercy, that thou wilt believe me, but
a plague break thy neck for frighting me! What's 35
become of the wenching rogues? I think they have
swallowed one another. I would laugh at that miracle.
Yet, in a sort, lechery eats itself. I'll seek them.

                                      Exit.

[Scene V. Another part of the plains.]

Enter Diomedes and Servant.

  Dio. Go, go, my servant, take thou Troilus' horse:
Present the fair steed to my lady Cressid.
Fellow, commend my service to her beauty:
Tell her I have chastised the amorous Trojan
And am her knight by proof. 5
  Ser.   I go, my lord.   *[Exit.]*

10. **beam:** lance. Shakespeare probably uses this word because he shared the general Elizabethan misconception that the Colossus of Rhodes had straddled the harbor and carried aloft a beacon light. See cut on p. 127.

11. **pashed corses:** smashed corpses.

15. **Sore:** grievously; **Sagittary:** a centaur (half horse, half man) who, in medieval versions of the Troy story, lent his skill with bow and arrows to the Trojan cause.

22. **lacks work:** finds no opponents.

23. **scaled sculls:** i.e., schools of fish.

24. **belching:** spouting.

25. **strawy:** like straws in being easily cut down, perhaps also in reference to their yellow hair.

27. **leaves and takes:** spares and kills.

30. **proof:** proven fact.

Enter Agamemnon.

Aga. Renew, renew! The fierce Polydamas
Hath beat down Menon. Bastard Margarelon
Hath Doreus prisoner
And stands Colossus-wise, waving his beam,　　　　　10
Upon the pashed corses of the kings
Epistrophus and Cedius. Polyxenes is slain;
Amphimachus and Thoas deadly hurt;
Patroclus ta'en or slain; and Palamedes
Sore hurt and bruised. The dreadful Sagittary　　　　15
Appals our numbers. Haste we, Diomed,
To reinforcement, or we perish all.

Enter Nestor.

Nes. Go, bear Patroclus' body to Achilles,
And bid the snail-paced Ajax arm for shame.
There is a thousand Hectors in the field.　　　　　20
Now here he fights on Galathe, his horse,
And there lacks work. Anon he's there afoot,
And there they fly or die, like scaled sculls
Before the belching whale. Then is he yonder,
And there the strawy Greeks, ripe for his edge,　　　25
Fall down before him, like a mower's swath.
Here, there, and everywhere he leaves and takes,
Dexterity so obeying appetite
That what he will he does, and does so much
That proof is called impossibility.　　　　　　30

37. **Crying on:** calling out the name of.
42. **forceless care:** i.e., careless care; recklessness.
49. **boy-queller:** boy-killer.

The Colossus of Rhodes as an artist conceived it in the sixteenth century. From André Thevet, *Cosmographie de Levant* (1554). (See [V.v.]10.)

Enter Ulysses.

Uly. Oh, courage, courage, princes! Great Achilles
Is arming, weeping, cursing, vowing vengeance.
Patroclus' wounds have roused his drowsy blood,
Together with his mangled Myrmidons,
That noseless, handless, hacked, and chipped come to   35
    him,
Crying on Hector. Ajax hath lost a friend
And foams at mouth, and he is armed and at it,
Roaring for Troilus, who hath done today
Mad and fantastic execution,   40
Engaging and redeeming of himself,
With such a careless force and forceless care,
As if that luck, in very spite of cunning,
Bade him win all.

Enter Ajax.

Ajax. Troilus! thou coward Troilus!   *Exit.* 45
Dio.   Ay, there, there.
Nes. So, so, we draw together.

Enter Achilles.

Achil.   Where is this Hector?
Come, come, thou boy-queller, show thy face!
Know what it is to meet Achilles angry.   50
Hector! where's Hector? I will none but Hector.
                    Exeunt.

[V.vi.] Ajax and Diomedes both seek Troilus, who appears and attacks the latter. Achilles comes upon Hector, who perceives that the Greek hero is winded and gives him a respite.

━━━━━━━━━━━━━━━━━━━━━━━

7. **that correction:** i.e., because he will see to the correction himself.

13. **look upon:** be a spectator.

14. **cogging:** cheating.

[Scene VI. Another part of the plains.]

Enter Ajax.

Ajax. Troilus, thou coward Troilus, show thy head!

Enter Diomedes.

Dio. Troilus, I say! where's Troilus?
Ajax.　　　　　　　　　　What wouldst thou?
Dio. I would correct him.
Ajax. Were I the general, thou shouldst have my　　5
  office
Ere that correction. Troilus, I say! what, Troilus!

Enter Troilus.

Tro. O traitor Diomed! Turn thy false face, thou
  traitor,
And pay thy life thou owest me for my horse.　　10
Dio. Ha, art thou there?
Ajax. I'll fight with him alone. Stand, Diomed!
Dio. He is my prize: I will not look upon.
Tro. Come, both, you cogging Greeks: have at you
  both!　　　　　　　　　[*Exeunt; fighting.*]　15

Enter Hector.

Hec. Yea, Troilus! Oh, well fought, my youngest
  brother!

19. **Pause:** rest.
21. **use:** practice.
22. **rest and negligence:** negligent inactivity.
33. **reck:** care.
37. **frush:** smash.

Enter Achilles.

Achil. Now do I see thee! Ha! have at thee, Hector!
Hec. Pause, if thou wilt.
    Achil. I do disdain thy courtesy, proud Trojan.   20
Be happy that my arms are out of use.
My rest and negligence befriends thee now,
But thou anon shalt hear of me again:
Till when, go seek thy fortune.   *Exit.*
    Hec.   Fare thee well.   25
I would have been much more a fresher man,
Had I expected thee.

Enter Troilus.

                How now, my brother!
    Tro. Ajax hath ta'en Aeneas. Shall it be?
No, by the flame of yonder glorious heaven,   30
He shall not carry him. I'll be ta'en too,
Or bring him off. Fate, hear me what I say!
I reck not though I end my life today.   *Exit.*

Enter one in armor.

    Hec. Stand, stand, thou Greek, thou art a goodly
    mark.   35
No? Wilt thou not? I like thy armor well:
I'll frush it, and unlock the rivets all,
But I'll be master of it. Wilt thou not, beast, abide?
Why then, fly on, I'll hunt thee for thy hide.
                    Exeunt.

[**V.vii.**] Achilles gathers his Myrmidons about him and orders them to surround Hector and fall upon him. Thersites witnesses a combat between Paris and Menelaus. He is challenged by a bastard son of Priam but dissuades him from attacking.

▬▬▬▬▬▬▬▬▬▬▬▬▬▬▬▬▬▬▬

5. **Empale:** surround, as with a paling fence.

10. **dog:** Thersites speaks like a spectator at a bull-baiting, urging now the bull, now the dog.

[Scene VII. Another part of the plains.]

Enter Achilles with Myrmidons.

Achil. Come here about me, you my Myrmidons.
Mark what I say. Attend me where I wheel.
Strike not a stroke, but keep yourselves in breath;
And when I have the bloody Hector found,
Empale him with your weapons round about.   5
In fellest manner execute your arms.
Follow me, sirs, and my proceedings eye.
It is decreed Hector the great must die.   *Exeunt.*

Enter Thersites: Menelaus and Paris, [fighting].

Ther. The cuckold and the cuckold-maker are at it.
Now, bull! now, dog! Loo, Paris, loo! Now my dou-   10
ble-horned Spartan! Loo, Paris, loo! The bull has the
game: ware horns, ho!   *Exeunt Paris and Menelaus.*

Enter [Margarelon, the] Bastard.

Mar. Turn, slave, and fight.
Ther. What are thou?
Mar. A bastard son of Priam's.   15
Ther. I am a bastard too. I love bastards. I am
bastard begot, bastard instructed, bastard in mind,
bastard in valor, in everything illegitimate. One bear
will not bite another, and wherefore should one

[V.viii.] Hector has just removed his helmet and hung up his shield when Achilles and his Myrmidons ambush him and hack him to death. Achilles ties the body of Hector to his horse's tail to drag it around the camp.

7. **vail:** sinking.
13. **amain:** with full strength of voice.

Impar Priamides dis congressus Achilli,
Irato cæsus Hector ab hoste cadit: 22. Heu decus Iliaci splendor et imperij.
Raptatur ægtli circum sua mœnia curru,

The combat between Hector and Achilles. From Isaac de la Rivière, *Speculum heroici* (1613).

131

bastard? Take heed, the quarrel's most ominous to   20
us. If the son of a whore fight for a whore, he tempts
judgment. Farewell, bastard.   [*Exit.*]

  Mar. The Devil take thee, coward!

                                       Exit.

[Scene VIII. Another part of the plains.]

Enter Hector.

  Hec. Most putrefied core, so fair without,
Thy goodly armor thus hath cost thy life.
Now is my day's work done. I'll take good breath.
Rest, sword! thou hast thy fill of blood and death.
[*Puts off his helmet and hangs his shield behind him.*]

Enter Achilles and Myrmidons.

  Achil. Look, Hector, how the sun begins to set;   5
How ugly night comes breathing at his heels.
Even with the vail and dark'ning of the sun
To close the day up, Hector's life is done.

  Hec. I am unarmed. Forego this vantage, Greek.

  Achil. Strike, fellows, strike: this is the man I seek.   10
                         [*Hector falls.*]
So, Ilion, fall thou next! Now, Troy, sink down!
Here lies thy heart, thy sinews, and thy bone.
On, Myrmidons! and cry you all amain,
"Achilles hath the mighty Hector slain."

                        Retreat [*sounded*].

19. **stickler-like:** like the stickler who umpired tournaments and parted the combatants.

20. **frankly:** freely.

21. **bait:** refreshment.

<hr>

[V.ix.] Word of the death of Hector at the hands of Achilles spreads in the Greek camp. Agamemnon concludes that if Hector is indeed slain, Troy is ready to fall.

<hr>

5. **bruit:** report.

Hark! a retire upon our Grecian part.   15
   Myr. The Trojan trumpets sound the like, my lord.
   Achil. The dragon wing of night o'erspreads the
     earth
And stickler-like the armies separates.
My half-supped sword, that frankly would have fed,   20
Pleased with this dainty bait, thus goes to bed.
                    [Sheathes his sword.]
Come, tie his body to my horse's tail;
Along the field I will the Trojan trail.
                         Exeunt.

[Scene IX. Another part of the plains.]

*Sound retreat. Shout. Enter Agamemnon, Ajax, Mene-
   laus, Nestor, Diomedes, and the rest, marching.*

   Aga. Hark! hark! what shout is that?
   Nes. Peace, drums!
   Sol. [*Within*] Achilles! Achilles! Hector's slain!
   Achilles!
   Dio. The bruit is, Hector's slain, and by Achilles.   5
   Ajax. If it be so, yet bragless let it be;
Great Hector was as good a man as he.
   Aga. March patiently along. Let one be sent
To pray Achilles see us at our tent.
If in his death the gods have us befriended,   10
Great Troy is ours, and our sharp wars are ended.
                         Exeunt.

[V.x.] Troilus reports Hector's death to Aeneas but vows defiance to the Greek army, and Diomedes in particular. Pandarus seeks Troilus' ear but is again brushed aside. He laments the sad fate of those who work on behalf of love and predicts that others of his profession will likewise suffer both the contempt and the diseases that afflict him.

████████████████████████████

9. **let your brief plagues be mercy:** show mercy in making your plagues quickly fatal.

14. **imminence:** imminent events.

15. **Address:** prepare.

20. **Niobes:** i.e., fountains. Niobe was a matron in Greek mythology whose pride in her many children incurred the anger of Apollo and Diana, who killed them all. In her tearful grief, Niobe changed to a stone that continued to weep.

[Scene X. Another part of the plains.]

Enter Aeneas, Paris, Antenor, and Deiphobus.

Aen. Stand, ho! yet are we masters of the field.
Never go home! Here starve we out the night.

Enter Troilus.

Tro. Hector is slain.
All.   Hector! The gods forbid!
Tro. He's dead and at the murderer's horse's tail   5
In beastly sort dragged through the shameful field.
Frown on, you Heavens, effect your rage with speed!
Sit, gods, upon your thrones, and smile at Troy!
I say at once, let your brief plagues be mercy,
And linger not our sure destructions on!   10
Aen. My lord, you do discomfort all the host.
Tro. You understand me not that tell me so.
I do not speak of flight, of fear, of death,
But dare all imminence that gods and men
Address their dangers in. Hector is gone.   15
Who shall tell Priam so, or Hecuba?
Let him that will a screech-owl aye be called
Go in to Troy and say there, "Hector's dead."
There is a word will Priam turn to stone,
Make wells and Niobes of the maids and wives,   20
Cold statues of the youth, and, in a word,
Scare Troy out of itself. But march away.

26. **Titan:** Helios, the sun-god, one of the Titans.

42. **verse:** i.e., in the Bible.

47-8. **painted cloths:** hangings containing painted pictures, often presenting a moral.

The destruction of Niobe's children by Apollo and Diana. From Gabriele Simeoni, *La vita et Metamorfoseo d'Ovidio* (1559). (See [V.x.]20.)

Hector is dead: there is no more to say.
Stay yet. You vile abominable tents,
Thus proudly pitcht upon our Phrygian plains,   25
Let Titan rise as early as he dare,
I'll through and through you! And, thou great-sized
        coward,
No space of earth shall sunder our two hates.
I'll haunt thee like a wicked conscience still,   30
That moldeth goblins swift as frenzy's thoughts.
Strike a free march to Troy! With comfort go.
Hope of revenge shall hide our inward woe.

                    [*As Troilus is going out, enter,
                    from the other side, Pandarus.*]

    Pan. But hear you, hear you!
    Tro. Hence, broker-lackey! ignomy and shame   35
Pursue thy life, and live aye with thy name!

                    Exeunt all but Pandarus.

    Pan. A goodly medicine for my aching bones! O
world! world! world! thus is the poor agent despised!
O traitors and bawds, how earnestly are you set
a-work, and how ill requited! Why should our en-   40
deavor be so loved and the performance so loathed?
What verse for it? What instance for it? Let me see:

    Full merrily the humblebee doth sing,
    Till he hath lost his honey and his sting;
    And, being once subdued in armed tail,   45
    Sweet honey and sweet notes together fail.

Good traders in the flesh, set this in your painted
cloths:

53. hold-door trade: i.e., procurers and prostitutes.

57. galled goose of Winchester: sufferer from syphilis acquired in one of the brothels owned by the Bishop of Winchester.

58. sweat: a feature of the treatment of syphilis.

As many as be here of Pandar's hall,
Your eyes, half out, weep out at Pandar's fall;   50
Or, if you cannot weep, yet give some groans,
Though not for me, yet for your aching bones.
Brethren and sisters of the hold-door trade,
Some two months hence my will shall here be
    made.   55
It should be now, but that my fear is this,
Some galled goose of Winchester would hiss.
Till then I'll sweat and seek about for eases,
And at that time bequeath you my diseases.

                              [*Exit.*]

Preface. This served as an advertisement in copies of the Quarto published in 1609, hinting that the play had either never been acted, or, if so, had not been cheapened by popular approval.

⁣⁣⁣⁣⁣⁣⁣⁣⁣⁣⁣⁣⁣⁣⁣⁣⁣⁣⁣⁣⁣⁣⁣⁣⁣⁣⁣⁣⁣⁣⁣⁣⁣⁣⁣⁣⁣⁣⁣

3. **passing:** surpassingly.

3-4. **palm comical:** prize for comedy.

4. **your:** a reference to the author.

7. **commodities:** profits.

8. **grand censors:** probably a reference to the aldermen of London, who disapproved of plays, and most of whom were businessmen.

A never writer to an ever reader: news

Eternal reader, you have here a new play, never
staled with the stage, never clapperclawed with the
palms of the vulgar, and yet passing full of the palm
comical; for it is a birth of your brain that never undertook anything comical vainly. And were but the   5
vain names of comedies changed for the titles of
commodities, or of plays for pleas, you should see all
those grand censors that now style them such vanities
flock to them for the main grace of their gravities;
especially this author's comedies, that are so framed   10
to the life that they serve for the most common commentaries of all the actions of our lives, showing such
a dexterity and power of wit that the most displeased
with plays are pleased with his comedies. And all
such dull and heavy-witted worldlings as were never   15
capable of the wit of a comedy, coming by report of
them to his representations, have found that wit there
that they never found in themselves and have parted
better witted than they came, feeling an edge of wit
set upon them more than ever they dreamed they had   20
brain to grind it on. So much and such savored salt
of wit is in his comedies that they seem (for their

27. testern: sixpence.

37-8. grand possessors: referring, probably, to the theatrical company, the King's Men at this time.

Venus, with a shell symbolizing her birth from .seafoam. From Vincenzo Cartari, *Imagini de gli dei delli antichi* (1615).

height of pleasure) to be born in that sea that
brought forth Venus. Amongst all there is none more
witty than this; and had I time I would comment   25
upon it, though I know it needs not (for so much as
will make you think your testern well bestowed), but
for so much worth as even poor I know to be stuffed
in it, it deserves such a labor as well as the best
comedy in Terence or Plautus. And believe this, that   30
when he is gone and his comedies out of sale, you
will scramble for them and set up a new English
Inquisition. Take this for a warning and, at the peril
of your pleasure's loss and judgments, refuse not nor
like this the less for not being sullied with the smoky   35
breath of the multitude; but thank fortune for the
scape it hath made amongst you, since by the grand
possessors' wills I believe you should have prayed for
them rather than been prayed. And so I leave all such
to be prayed for (for the states of their wit's healths)   40
that will not praise it.

Vale.

The Heavens themselves, the planets, and this center
Observe degree, priority, and place.
[*Ulysses*—I.[iii.]89-90]

Oh, when degree is shaked,
Which is the ladder to all high designs,
The enterprise is sick! [*Ulysses*—I.[iii.]105-7]

Take but degree away, untune that string,
And hark what discord follows. [*Ulysses*—I.[iii.]113-14]

Like a strutting player—whose conceit
Lies in his hamstring, and doth think it rich
To hear the wooden dialogue and sound
'Twixt his stretched footing and the scaffoldage.
[*Ulysses*—I.[iii.]157-60]

Pride is his own glass, his own trumpet.
[*Agamemnon*—[II.iii.]156]

To fear the worst oft cures the worse.
[*Cressida*—[III.ii.]71]

This is the monstruosity in love, lady, that the
will is infinite and the execution confined.
[*Troilus*—[III.ii.]79-80]

To be wise and love
Exceeds man's might: that dwells with gods above.
[*Cressida*—[III.ii.]157-58]

Time hath, my lord, a wallet at his back
Wherein he puts alms for oblivion.
[*Ulysses*—[III.iii.]154-55]

Love, friendship, charity, are subjects all
To envious and calumniating Time.
[*Ulysses*—[III.iii.]184-85]

One touch of nature makes the whole world kin.
[*Ulysses*—[III.iii.]186]

The grief is fine, full, perfect, that I taste.
[*Cressida*—[IV. iv.]3]

Injurious Time now with a robber's haste
Crams his rich thiev'ry up, he knows not how.
[*Troilus*—[IV. iv.]43-4]

There's language in her eye, her cheek, her lip,
Nay, her foot speaks. Her wanton spirits look out
At every joint and motive of her body.
[*Ulysses*—[IV. v.]64-6]

What's past and what's to come is strewed with husks
And formless ruin of oblivion.
[*Agamemnon*—[IV. v.]184-85]

  The end crowns all,
And that old common arbitrator, Time,
Will one day end it.   [*Hector*—[IV. v.]249-51]